Plague Year

ALSO BY PETER ABBOT

Librarian
Gukurahundi: Voice of the Lord
Hamiltonians
Armistice
Quintet

Plague Year

A Novel

Peter Abbot

Rock's Mills Press
Oakville, Ontario
2021

Published by
Rock's Mills Press
www.rocksmillspress.com

The first section of this novel, "Quintet," was published as a standalone
novella in 2020.

For information about this book, please contact us at
customer.service@rocksmillspress.com

CONTENTS

... the deadly pestilence ... started in the East ... and it killed an infinite number of people....

Without pause it spread from one place and it stretched its miserable length over the West.

And against this pestilence no human wisdom or foresight was of any avail ... not only did talking to or being around the sick bring infection and a common death, but also touching the clothes of the sick or anything touched or used by them ...

There were some people who ... gathered in small groups and lived entirely apart ... spending their time with music and other pleasures....

—Giovanni Boccaccio (1313–1375), *The Decameron*

... the infection spread in a dreadful manner ... the richer sort of people thronged out of town....

I had two important things before me: the one was carrying on my business ... and the other was the preservation of my life in so dismal a calamity as I saw apparently was comping upon the whole city.

... the best preparation for the plague was to run away from it....

... I resolved that I would stay in town.

We are all in this craft and must sink or swim together.

—Daniel Defoe, *A Journal of the Plague Year*, 1722

QUINTET

ONE

Tuesday 31st March 2020
BORIS

Even the date seems like an ending. (End of WINTER!) But it's also a BEGINNING! (Beginning of SPRING!)

For several weeks now (how many? I'm already forgetting, and I guess that's not only my advanced age, 84, asserting itself, it's probably true of most of us, here in Canada, in my generation – we will be another Lost Generation and deserve to be, though I pray we don't take succeeding generations down with us – or maybe I do pray for that, for the end of Humanity – when I am able to believe, very temporarily and against all evidence, in the existence of God? A God who CARES – not merely atoms –)

And you see already, you who are reading this, that I am a confused old man. Gerontion? So why read what I write? (Don't BOTHER if you have something better to do!) (Actually I know I'm writing this for MYSELF alone – killing Time while waiting for DEATH? – though of course I know well enough that we don't ever kill Time, Time kills US, always has, always will!) (Did we Humans, we endlessly reproducing Humans, generally have a Good Time? Until it became a very Bad Time?) No doubt I am all too representative of the pullulating millions who have for so long been wrecking this planet. (I told them how it had to end!) It'll be like reading yourself out. (What does that mean?) Music is preferable, always has been. (Which is why I'm half-listening to a CD – Schubert's 'Unfinished Symphony' – Ha! Schubert, Schubert,

1

if we can't perform your great Quintet – well, I'll play it again, later, again and again! My favourite CD. And your music CAN never finish – never!) (Oh – until WE do.) And if WE survive, our Lark Quartet-plus-One will perform that great-est-masterpiece with fervor, with gratitude, with JOY. With or without an audience. But definitely with its Founding Cellist! Yes, at least I am that! WOT LARKS!!!

JENNIFER – we were so glad to welcome her at the run-through of the Quintet – when we were expecting to perform it quite soon afterwards. Then, of course, the Plague burst upon us and is changing everything, EVERYTHING! We were forced to cancel the performance, as we all know. But I am living with the hope that we still may be able to rehearse and perform that glorious masterpiece one day! So – I was also about to tell her, Jennifer, and will, that we have a new custom (!), of sending emails to each other, to keep in touch – all of the members to send me a copy of their emails, when we are rehearsing or performing, and I will choose one every day and send it to all of you – This started as a JOKE but then I realized it was useful, we are a very close little musical group, as you'll discover, and it will be not only a good way to keep in touch and get to know each other, as a close group of musi-cal builders rearing our "PALACE OF MUSIC"!!! We will try to be completely open with each other, no shame, no con-cealment – naked and unashamed! "Sorrow is hard to bear, and doubt is slow to clear … / But God has a few of us whom he whispers in the ear; / The rest may reason and welcome: 'tis we musicians know."

For several weeks (as I was saying before, as I HAVE said, haven't I?) that Plague named COVID-19 (or Coronavirus? – which is it? or has that ceased to matter? What's in a name? – Names change, a rose by any other name – etc – BUT this ain't no rose! – NO, NO – THIS Plague is ravaging our planet. *Our* planet? We fucked you up, Earth. You were never OURS, but we used you as if we owned you, we ABused you! and now–) Yes – this Plague, this Pestilence, now destroying many many MANY human-beings, MILLIONS? in many many countries, starting in China, where it all began anyway, a few months ago – (China, where a few million citizens won't be missed? But would ANY of us be missed? After a few years?) Yes, where it all began, just a few months ago, in China, yes, as this joyful New Year of 2020 was also just beginning –

And I am an old man, as I was just saying – wasn't I? (84!) – and old people are apparently its preferred (COVIDED!) victims (yes, because the most CULPABLE, and most HELPLESS?) – so many of us dying now in our so-called seniors' homes – Definitely a majority of victims are Seniors, they say – OLD PEOPLE like me – most of us likely to die anyway before long, as a natural consequence of hosting several diseases that are (even as I type this!) feeding on our bodies – and our minds too, yes, CANCER and the dreaded ALZHEIMER'S above all.

Sorry, I am rampaging again!

She's calling me – Alice, I mean – calling me for supper. So, get up, old man, OLD MAN! – time to totter carefully, slowly, so SLOWLY, downstairs. Before she has to shout again. You are one of the fortunate ones, Boris! (And she's a good cook.) But think of all those in old-folks' homes ('seniors' homes' I should say) – think of how imprisoned they must be feeling – I really must telephone Archie tomorrow morning. (I did try, and failed, this morning.)

SO, to each of you fellow members of a great Quartet, I have set you an example of UTTER OPENNESS!! Your turn now!

Wednesday 1st April 2020
JAMES

Another day without Ken. Stupid! – you *were* stupid, James. Why get so angry over such a small disagreement? And where is he now? I guess he'll want to punish me – but it's dangerous now, none of us can ignore the danger. Ken! Please don't be getting drunk in a bar. Please come back – or at least phone or email me, please, please –

But I'm talking to myself. I'll email the others maybe, the Four I mean. Jennifer & I would have gotten to know each other by now – the extra cellist – but we didn't get beyond our first run-through before the Govt began closing almost every-thing down – a few weeks ago, how fast the time goes! I guess that was necessary, most people seem to think so – govern-ments in most countries are doing it –

I'm feeling like a prisoner – well, I guess most of the pop-ulation of this city feel that way. And citizens all round the world! How easily & casually we just went about our lives, working in our offices during the day, visiting friends in the evening, restaurants, pubs, watching TV or going to a show – Of course all the shows are cancelled now, & all sporting events, even the Olympics. Never thought I'd miss the Office – though problems accumulated there – & many angry clients – once the airlines started cancelling flights, & of course the cruise-ships, I think some of them are still stuck out at sea with a load of sick passengers & others who aren't & just want to be home – looks as if the whole Cruise industry is dead already, or dying – maybe even other travelling won't happen much in future & then what will I –?

In yesterday's local newspaper: "We're in a race against time" (headline) & "COVID-19 continues to spread as new travel restrictions imposed" (by Govt). April Fool's Day! For us all. Believe nothing, go back to sleep & dream happy dreams, you Fool!

Why do I go on rambling like this? An old habit – does it actually help to record disordered thoughts & feelings? – & then not even to look again, ever, at what I wasted time writing! Words, words! But it's deeds that matter now – & music, the soul needs music, & not only the soul – my brain, my emotions, even my muscles are twitching – That concert, yes of course it was cancelled, like everything else, weeks ago, & I was specially looking forward to it. The Schubert Quintet in C! My Mother loved it, *loved* it, & so do I, I always did – it's partly why I chose to learn the violin! & so does – oh Ken. Please.

So I'll send out another of my urgent emails – "KEN, I LOVE YOU, PLEASE COME HOME". (Boris, *are* you *reading* this? Are any of you?) (*Your* crazy idea, Boris!) (So now, pay attention!)

I wonder if this will work? This scheme that Boris has imposed on us, on all the members of the Quartet. Seems crazy, as I say! And on No. 5 as well, the second cello. Jennifer – are you reading this? You're only temporary of course, just for the Schubert Quintet that we were scheduled to perform before the Pandemic shut everything down. But Boris insists that we *will* perform the Quintet this summer! Crazy! Why the insistence, Boris? And that we each send him a daily diary-entry from now on, & he will choose one to represent each day, & they will accumulate into a record of our lives as we rehearse. Crazy idea! But you were always crazy, Boris. *You* said that! So you can choose me to represent today – after all, it's April Fool's Day, & I'm the Fool – so, as they say, ENJOY! Enjoy my discomfort, my pain, all of you. Laugh at me! My turn will come! (If you play fair, Sir!) (Remember, you said "Totally honest & open!")

Thursday 2nd April 2020
ANNA
What a glorious day! Well, it's not, of course, in the context of what we are all enduring, this COVID-19 PANDEMIC that's terrifying us all; but it is, otherwise, so gloriously bright and sunny that you just long to be out there in the Park! When I went out onto the balcony for a few minutes, with my coffee, just very briefly, I could see only one moving figure on the Park path, a young man in shorts (in SHORTS!) running along the main path. Otherwise hardly any movement, even along the street: only two cars, and nobody, NOBODY, walking along the sidewalk. You feel as if you're on the moon!

Myrna, are you there? Still in bed? Surely not.

Main headline in today's newspaper: "Surge anticipated in next three weeks". Surge of what? COVID-19 patients, what else? And helpful articles about local education, like "Now is the time to focus on what really matters – not the school year"! I wonder about all my kids. Some of them will be doing the work I put on the website, especially if their Mothers push them, like that Mrs. Cohen; but the immigrant kids, or the two refugee kids; and I wonder what their parents are doing, if they still have jobs? Well, I can't help there, can I? But I'll try to call the School after breakfast and find out what's happening. It's good that Trudeau and the Government are doing something about the economy: apparently so many Canadians are in financial difficulty, not being able to pay their rent this month or whatever. Worrying; what a mess!

I read an article somewhere, the other day, about keeping

a diary: how helpful to be doing that in this period when COVID-19 is making us stay indoors. So it's good that I have always kept one! And especially now that Boris has again demanded that we forward each entry to him. Why? But I could hardly refuse! (Well, I will refuse if you are just playing a game with us, Sir!)

Friday 3rd April 2020
JENNY

I'm surprised that the newspaper is still being delivered. I must try to thank the newsboy – if I talk to him from this side of the front-door, surely I would be far enough away, but maybe I shouldn't give him a tip – they say that type of physical contact could transmit the virus or whatever it is – but at least I could say Thank You at arm's length, surely? I wonder when he delivers the newspaper? Probably too early for me to get to the front-door, maybe I should pin a thank-you note to the screen-door? But if he stops delivery, I wouldn't really miss it – the CBC News on the radio is enough, *more* than enough, these days, I think! In fact, there's a *lot* of things that clutter one's life which, I confess, I wouldn't really miss.

But what a shock when I did read the newspaper – I saw the main headline, "We're in a race against time", so then I read, in the end, almost everything there – and as I say, what a shock to see how the whole COVID-19 situation, here in Hamilton, is much *much* more serious than I knew. I must call Sheila tonight in case they don't know up there in Cottage Country! An article on the front page is entitled "COVID-19 continues to spread as new travel restrictions imposed" and in the article it says "Ontario reported its largest single-day increase by far … 351 new COVID-19 cases and ten more deaths Monday, the province's largest single-day increase by far, as Premier Doug Ford warned that a shortage of critical medical supplies may be perilously close..." That disturbed me all day on and off – I could hardly concentrate on what I was reading – and then on TV in the evening, the news under the screen had this: "80K COVID-19 CASES IN ONT. BY APRIL 30" – and in the American news in the CBC newscast, "Trump orders US Company to stop exporting masks to Canada" – just when it seems wearing a mask – I haven't got one – is likely to become mandatory even in the super-market. As I say, all a shock to me, and no doubt to many Canadians.

And it's a real pity about the Schubert Quintet, I was really looking forward to that – the rehearsals and the three performances – they're such a good Quartet, one of the best, otherwise they wouldn't be in such demand to go on tours in Europe as well as Canada. I was lucky to be invited because they needed an extra cello for the Schubert – which I love! It was Anna who arranged the invitation, I think – she has played Second Violin in the Quartet for quite a few years, and I know that Boris, who started it after he came to Canada with his parents, all those years ago – they were refugees, I think – has said how much he admires her playing, he told me that – I had a sort of interview with him, he's an old man and he did make some strange comments, I thought – Anna said he had been a refugee from I think she said Hungary and came to Canada as a boy or young man, with his parents who had been members of a major orchestra. He has a strong accent! But I had no problem understanding him. He's tough, I think, and of course he has very high standards. I played movements from Bach, the third cello suite, which I have always loved, and he grunted and said I'd "do". (Hope I haven't offended you, Sir, by writing down my thoughts just as they were – but you did say to write down honestly whatever I was thinking!

So that's what I'm doing!)

(Also, it's good in a way, I think, that I have time now, with this shut-in situation we're all in, to write down things I would otherwise forget!)

Saturday 4th April 2020
KEN

You there, James? Were you wondering about me – what I did, where I went, after I walked out on April Fool's Day? See, you don't know much about me, do you? I always said that, didn't I? I always came way down at the bottom of your attention. Your interest. I always said that. I'm BORING! You never paid attention and I doubt if you will now. Anyway, I'm coming back later today. It's *my* apartment, or *was*, wasn't it? I PAY THE RENT. You are MY GUEST, and anyway you only care about playing your bloody fiddle! I mean, apart from making-out with any passing Bunny. Oh and the World of Travel. You were into Cruises and now all that might be gone – so many cruise-ships and their contents stuck out at sea because no port wants to let their passengers on land distributing a plague! Surprise! So who will risk going on a cruise in future? – Oh well, doesn't matter. YOU don't matter. And obviously I DON'T MATTER to you! Just useful that my apartment is in the Village. "So convenient" you said. Well, it is – but remember, I pay the rent. You have your own place – remember?

Dan – Remember him? You sneered that I let him pick me up in the Workhorse. Well, that's who I've been with for a week. Other side of TO. Better believe it! We've had a real good time together. Said he wants me to come back and live permanently with him! He has to go and see about his Father first. Who's in a Home, I think I told you that. But now the

9

Home is closing – four deaths from that COVID or whatever-it's-called. So they emailed him. The Home has to close down! Dan says he thinks his cousin will look after him, but if not he will have to bring him back here.

So that's how things are. Dan will be leaving soon. He's going by train, if it's operating, and if it isn't he'll have to go by bus. He's trying to find out right now, but they aren't answering. Just a message to try again later, he says. I'll be leaving when he does. With a suitable gap between us, of course. He has a reputation to protect! Unlike feckless musicians, banker-types must dress well and behave better!

I've been reading the newspaper while I'm waiting. Shock! It says, I'm quoting, "Canada's most populous province" that's us of course "could see between 3,000 to 15,000 deaths because of COVID, according to predictions from Ontario public health officials." *15,000!* And the Mayor said that *over 1,600 could be dead by the end of this month!* "That is 50 a day or that is two people every hour." Wow. Think about that! Yet some people are still getting together in big groups, for parties, even when it's against the law now. I've seen that, really stupid behaviour! People are getting nervous and officious. Yesterday when I went for a walk, someone shouted at me, bloody fool! – but you got to get SOME exercise. I'm already – Hope the buses are still running. If not, you may not see me ever again! EVER!!!

Anyway, here's Dan. Says he's ordered a taxi and it can take me home after it drops him off at the station. So I'll send this to you now. So I'll see you soon. And I hope you will have read this by then and will be ready for me. My great Comeback!

TWO

What a glorious day! How I would have enjoyed a walk in the Park and by the Lake! The dog along the street has been barking again – I hope it's not imprisoned indoors, like the one that was kept in next-door's basement through most of last year – I can't bear cruelty to animals!

But I'm rambling, Anna. Sorry. It was good to have that chat last night & know that we are both still alive! I'm so glad I decided to telephone – though I wondered if that was allowed. So many things we aren't allowed to do now – or *must* do, like washing & washing & *washing* one's hands. It reminds me of being a schoolgirl in England again! And I wonder how the kids I teach, taught, will manage! I must try to talk to all of them today on my iPhone & see how they are getting on. Poor kids! But they'll have to get used to it. This could be their Future! How do you feel about it? Same as me? I wonder if they'll be more rambunctious when this is all over? If it ever is! Or quieter, calmer?

Anna, did you listen to the Queen's Address this afternoon? It was on CBC TV. Very inspiring. I should have mentioned it when we talked last night. She's 93! Even older than Boris!! Didn't he say he's 83? – when he was congratulating himself, at that first & so-far-only read-through Schubert rehearsal? Queenie quoted Vera Lynn, "We'll meet again." "Don't know where, don't know when"! My Mother used to sing that. She was a child during the War, in England. She was a Vackie, sent to the Midlands somewhere, a farm, she hated that, but she also said it probably saved her life. My Dad, he was much older than her, & he fought in North Africa, but he

11

wouldn't ever talk about that, or anything about the War, "Better forgotten" he'd say. Sorry, I'm rambling. I was telling you about the Queen's Address. She also said "Better days will return" & "We will succeed". Of course it's her job to cheer us up! They even showed a clip of her & her little sister Princess Margaret giving a talk during the War, cheering up other children of England & the Empire. But I should also say that, before the Queen came on, the CBC said that 5,000 people have already died of what's-it, COVID-19, *already*, in the U.K. Which is frightening, isn't it?

It was such a lovely morning, & I was just longing to go out walking!

You asked me if I'd like to be in England now, & I said I'd think about it. No, I don't think so. Did I tell you I'm an only child? And both my parents died some time ago, my mother was killed when I was a small girl, she was knocked down by a speeding car, it was terrible, I can't really talk about it, I don't want to think about it. And my father, he fell to pieces, so I was brought up by my aunt, & the only good thing was that she was a cellist, quite a famous cellist really, & she taught me – Aunt Emily, she was a lovely kind person, & a teacher, so I suppose that's why I am a teacher – & a cellist, I love the cello, you know that. But I *despise* the violin, such a thin screechy sound! Oh, I'm teasing you, Anna! Boris said to write freely, just what we are feeling, so blame him when I insult you!!!

I wish we could get together. We're both lonely, aren't we? Or at least *I* am.

Monday 6th April 2020
BORIS

News that the British Prime Minister who has had COVID for a while is now in Special Care, is that what they call it? In a London hospital. I wonder how seriously ill he is? Anyway, he'll get the best care possible, so if he doesn't make it, gloom will definitely spread through the UK. Maybe won't be much better over here – in New York, latest news very serious! Trump has jumped again, from denying that they have a problem, to saying Yes, they do have a problem, but of course he is on TOP of it, he will SAVE AMERICA!!!! – but of course, and everyone knows this except for his Supporters, he will just claim that he was right, whatever situation develops! The TRUTH means nothing to him – as we all know now.

But why bother with Trump? Alice, where art thou? Your ancient decrepit husband needs FOOD! Before he settles into his after-lunch nap. (I wonder if the Queen takes a nap? She's a real trooper, that was a great speech she gave on TV yesterday! She was calm, consoling, helpful, even *hopeful*. I think a lot of her audience would have been as impressed as I was! Of course she would be protected from any chance of that virus getting into HER system, but she wasn't always so protected – especially during the War, I think, or when she went travelling in other countries.) And look at what we've heard on this evening's news, that the British Prime Minister is in Hospital now, with that COVID-19! Will he survive? If he doesn't, could be a panic in the whole population of England!! Tense days!

Ah, I hear Alice. Soon she'll appear with my dinner. I don't feel very hungry but I should eat. (In my earlier, conducting days, I was a big eater – and DISCRIMINATING, all those superb restaurants, when I was First Cello in the LSO, that was the life!!!) And then Alice, I should have avoided romance, she wasn't even a very good pianist – but she offered to accompany me, when I needed to prepare, and that was It!! Sometimes I've thought that she trapped me into marriage – and then didn't even produce children! But she looks after me now, we are two old friends heading for the Exit, hand in hand! (Are you reading this, my dear? Of course not, you are not a Member of the Quartet. So am I talking to myself! And I haven't been the best husband, have I? Or have I?) (Dear Readers, do not be shocked by my levity. Alice knows, I hope, that I love her.)

Now I'm back for a final contribution to today's record. After my after-lunch snooze. (Who will read it when I'm gone, or even value it? My journal. I thought of leaving it to the National Gallery or, if they don't want it – they didn't want the diary of a fine composer I knew! – to a University Collection. DIARY OF A MUSICAL GENIUS WHO WAS ALSO A WAR-REFUGEE!!!! But now, even if we survive, and even if the survivors value classical music – who knows? This record, of our thoughts and activities might be – And I am contradicting myself, I think. Who was it said "If I wish to contradict myself, I'll contradict myself!" (NOT Trump, long before him, but same type of human-being!) As Alice once said, woundingly, keeping a diary is just your little time-wasting hobby. That did hurt, my dear – you knew it would hurt!)

Our newspaper's main headline: "Outbreak at retirement home escalates" – "Thirteen residents and five staff … have COVID-19". And another front-page article: "Ontario COVID-19 deaths jump past 100". Hard not to be depressed. And on TV, a discussion about how demanding and depressing, and dangerous, daily work is for the doctors and nurses who tend hospital patients. They also need more surgical masks, and apparently our great noble friendly neighbour to the South has stopped them being sent here, they are only for REPUBLICAN AMERICANS?

That young cellist, who Anna recommended as second cellist, for the Schubert, telephoned me last night, apparently for a chat. Alice told me she's probably frightened and needed a shoulder to cry on – well, maybe she did, and I did talk to her for a while, but I hope she won't make a habit of this. It was Anna who brought her in, and she *is* quite a good cellist, I agree. But I am NOT a good SUGAR-DADDY, having had no practice, that's what I told Alice – who clearly thought I was somehow criticizing *her*! Oh well, time for bed. I wonder if these diary-bits *are* a good idea? Maybe, like that email stuff the young do, they encourage one to throw aside barriers of politeness and honesty. (Or so I hope!!!)

I can still pray, I find, even though my prayers have no recipient.

"Gentle Jesus, meek & mild"? But your bad Daddy has it in for us! "The Lord is my shepherd …" Yes, and we are Your sheep!

Tuesday 7th April 2020
KEN

So I'm back! Not that my Beloved seems to care – are you listening, Jimmy-boy? But I know who *is* listening, while he lies there, basking in our total subservience, our love, love, love – he will even purr while plotting evil against us, won't you? – (No, not you, dear Boris!) Oh Pusska, almighty Pusska, if you harbor this disease that's killing us humans, please accept our total submission and remember where your milk and sustenance come from. Besides, we adore you, as I was saying. Surely it's only Tigers, like that one in the news, who fall victim to COVID-19. Among animals, I mean. And they are far away, in India or zoos.

Oh, James, I am so BORED already. Maybe I need to run

off again. James, are you listening? You may be First Violin, but Schubert loved the viola. *Loved* it! He was *passionate* about the viola, you can hear that – the recording that Boris sent each of us, which may not be the *perfect* interpretation of the Quintet, tells us that our lovely Schubert, whatever his other fancies and proclivities, and apparently he was a very good boy, though how did he get syphilis, then? – but he loved the VIOLA. And *I* love the viola. And if you ever again cast aspersions on it, even in a joke, my dear old James, I will smash your effete instrument, your commonplace little violin, into a million fragments!

And I don't think you even bother to read my emails, do you? If you do – well, you don't. (But Other People will!)

And I don't think, to be completely honest, that I can settle to reading any of those Jane Austens you keep on recommending. Shakespeare? Maybe – one of the comedies? But not now, not today.

So. I'll do my washing. I'll read the newspaper (must keep up with the news – all about COVID, as if nothing else was happening, *anywhere*). Oh, there's the British PM, fighting for his life, as they say, even if he is just lying there, unable to speak or think, poor man. He may have been the Ultimate Bastard, ruining his country by pulling it out of Europe – but as PM he is clearly extra-precious now and far above the lives and feelings of his subjects, let them eat cake! Am I merely mean – as you once said, do you recall that quarrel? – when we first started being together? You said I had no feelings!

It's a grey day today – "disconsolate" is the word that comes to my mind. And still a bit cool. I went out onto the balcony for a short while, just to get some fresh (?) air – hardly any traffic, the odd car or bus, or police cruiser – but, over in the park, that madman, running, running – in shorts!!!

Nothing stops him. Or ever will. Except (whisper it) Death.

4:30   Yes, Death is now our neighbor. Maybe one day, quite soon, we will be able to laugh, or at least smile, remembering our fears. Or maybe not. Tonight on CBC I notice that the final appearance of *Schitt's Creek* is scheduled; I intend to watch (you too?), I never had more than a glimpse of it earlier (too busy? No, just never connected), but apparently it's been a worldwide success, so one ought to bow down & worship. I'm not really joking – Trumptrash has just been trampling us again, I'm sure you noticed, ordering a company that makes Masks to cease fulfilling any Canadian orders, so – Apparently that's over now, that skirmish, though there will be more – why does he hate Trudeau? Because he's young and pretty? Or because we're too weak up here to matter? When he has those Dictator friends –

Oh, James, please let's not connect only thisaway – it's time to forgive me, your Peppy Playboy, you once called me that, remember? – So *please!* See, I'm begging – I who, I mean whom, you also once called Ultimate Snob. (I'm *not* a snob!) We can't go on like this – & especially *now* when the world's falling apart & we are all threatened. Wonder if our dear Schubert felt like this when he knew his time was going, going – but, before it was gone, the glory of that Quintet!!! – we *must* play it, if only as our apotheosis. And *then*, Master Death, you can take us. James, WE ARE FRIENDS!!! Remember?

Wednesday 8th April 2020
ANNA

Another grey day! What are you up to, my dear Second Cellist? Something more noble than washing your smalls, I hope; or making a list for a quick shop, for basic survival requirements like bread and milk. I'm already getting edgy. Did I tell you that I once had a stay in hospital with extreme depression, when I was a university student. I hated it; in fact that reaction is what ultimately saved me, I think – hating it. All I wanted was to get out of there, and I had enough sense left to see that only obedience and smiles would accomplish that! So I became a failed nurse, and then a music-teacher! Teaching kids to love Schubert (I hope)!

You said you were lonely, Jenny? Wonder if we could get together, if only for a short while? But no doubt that is *verboten* too. There was a list on the radio, CBC, this morning, of things one *mustn't do*, but I didn't listen carefully. Did you? Please email me back anyway! And I will call you this evening, it was lovely to hear your voice and to have that conversation. We're lucky these days to have both the telephone, for chats, and also the iPhone etc. I tell that to my kids, warning them about the internet and to be careful what they write in emails; though I guess you can also be recorded on the telephone? So just be careful about what you say, which is good anyway! They are undisciplined!

Sorry, I'm just rambling. Did you watch "Schitt's Creek" last night? A lot of self-congratulating went on. I shouldn't really have wasted my time, except that one has so much time to waste now! And I was tired of reading. But something I saw in this morning's newspaper (I wonder how long that will continue now, delivery of the paper I mean) was that Bill Withers has died. He was 81, almost as old as Boris, but he had retired long ago, Bill Withers; you may not have heard of him, but you may have heard a song of his, I loved it, I can hear him in my memory, his lovely warm voice, singing it: "Lean on Me", do you know it? When I was – I just told you about my depression when I was a student, maybe I was thinking about that, I mean because of that item about Bill Withers dying. I loved that song, and I had it on a tape that I would play and play until it wore out. Oh, sorry, Jenny, I guess I'm just – but I'm being self-indulgent and unfair to you. What else? I'm reading a lovely novel. I'll tell you about it later, when I've finished it.

Did you notice in yesterday's newspaper – ? Maybe you don't get it. There was a long article on the cholera epidemic in Hamilton, in 1854. It said that at least 550 people died, out of the city's population of less than 20,000; and that was after an earlier epidemic, in 1832, that was "also disastrous". The newspaper also reported that the number of Americans who have died so far in our COVID-19 has now reached 12,000, with 350,000 confirmed infections. But yesterday the paper said "COVID-19 DEATHS LEVEL OFF IN NEW YORK". A massive number of protective masks now in use or on order, but "medical masks are in short supply" and we are being urged to make our own masks, to wear when we go shopping! Why do I keep noting facts and figures? Well, they do concern the survival of our fellow human-beings, and include us truly, though I must say that just trying to think about all of this is truly mind-stretching and depressing. I wonder if any experts are now saying or thinking "Over-population." But then what difference would that make – in a situation when, clearly, the world's population might be decimated? Would the disappearance of humans be beneficial for all other creatures? I never asked you – are you religious? Do you go to church?

I am not good at thinking out things, Jenny. I think you are better at that. Maybe it helps being younger. You probably guessed, from my grey hair, I am in my fifties, and semi-retired. Just an old school-marm! You'd probably not like to talk about teaching; especially now. But we both love music!

I'll telephone you for a chat this evening. If you don't want that, just tell me. I won't be offended! If only we could get together. We could play duets? My piano's in tune. Or we could listen to some of my CDs; and I could offer tea and cookies etc! By the way, I think Boris gave all of us copies of that CD of the Schubert String Quintet, as performed by the Weller Quartet? I hope you have it too? A good performance, he told me. "Listen carefully to that! But *we* can do better!" The two of us – We could listen to it, and play our parts, as practice, with it. And I have other CDs that you might enjoy; we could listen together.

I'll sign off now, Jenny. Would you mind if I call you Jennifer? I feel more comfortable with full names. I have the CBC News on, I was half-listening to that wonderful Organ Symphony by Saint Saens (have I spelt that right?); but then the News came on and they have just said that the number of COVID deaths in England today is almost one thousand! And their Prime Minister is still in hospital with that disease. And how many more deaths have occurred in Ontario and the rest of Canada? Oh, where will this end? So troubling – if only one could stop thinking about it! But it's wrecking our lives.

Thursday 9th April
JAMES

Oh, oh, oh, oh. Every morning the reports of COVID-19 deaths in Canada and of course around the world are worse. And it's Maundy Thursday today (do you know that, my dear Pagan?), a sunny windy day, Springlike, clearing away cobwebs and dust (Good Friday tomorrow – that will feel timely for Christians around the world, maybe? – & then Easter Sunday) – & 20,000 cases in Canada, 500 deaths, 2 million infected, 400,000 jobs lost in Ontario alone, & so on & so on

… Awful, ugly facts accumulating. What are we going to do, Ken? Let's be very serious, very mature for once, and think it out together. No more fucking about. I am thinking that, for a start, you should come here so we can work things out together, live together permanently or semi-permanently. Then you won't be able to go on accusing me of trying to take over your apartment! This house is too big for me – I should never have inherited it – or I should have sold it immediately & bought myself a condo right in the Gay Village. And all possibility of daily work is gone, as you know – no cruises, no travelling abroad or even in Canada, & surely your mysterious travel & financial activities are gone too – aren't they? "Nevermore!" Cruise-ships are dead, & probably airlines too. (Oh, but maybe your Income Tax stuff? Time for that. But will it still happen? Nothing is as it was! But you have so many irons in your fire, so to speak! – No, take that how you like – no further comment! Trudeau will surely legislate a tax delay? I'm trying to be serious, and you should help me!)

Do you ever read Agony Aunt stuff? Me neither, but in this morning's paper, I guess because there was time to sit & read it through, this headline caught my eye: "Single, frightened amid global pandemic". And is that *me*? To be honest – maybe. I thought Maybe. Anyway, the letter started like this: "I'm 42, single, live alone & I'm scared." And I, James Blair, am 37, single, live alone, & – "I can't visit my parents because they're elderly and health-compromised, I can't visit my brother who lives out of town" & doesn't want to know anyway! And finally "I work, read, go out only for groceries & other essentials & eat alone. The news frightens me more every day…. I have no relationships at all now, & I'm not even sure why I'm writing this." So then I sat there, at the kitchen table, for a while, drinking coffee & reading the newspaper &

thinking, and Pusska eventually jumped up onto me to ask if I was still alive. AM I still alive, Ken? Are YOU? How much longer have we got? Are we friends or enemies? And also my Mother, I think I told you she's frail, in a Home other side of Toronto, I haven't visited her, & maybe neither have my sister & brother, though they put her there – I haven't talked to them since they attacked me for being gay ten years ago, at my Father's funeral. But my Mother – how could I forget her, even if she betrayed me – as I said, I just haven't visited her, maybe she's already dead, maybe the Home she's in is one of those in the news, decimated by the virus? So – well, you see why I'm a mess? – All that, just from reading a letter to an agony-aunt! But, Ken. Let's talk. Really talk. Please. Maybe there's not much time left.

I should stop writing emails to you. We should talk. You should come & live with me. PLEASE TELEPHONE. I don't plan on going out tonight (!!!).

THREE

Friday 10th April 2020
BORIS

Sun and wind (*very* windy; I hear it whistling round this big old house, looking for a way in!). And it's Good Friday! I'm going to listen, yet again, to the CD of the Schubert Quintet (I've provided them all with that), it inspires and consoles me – but before that I'll listen to that Haydn Quartet, the one that superbly transmutes Christ's suffering into a series of variations. (Of course I'm not a Christian, but I do recognize the horror of tortures like that crucifixion.) And after that, yes, the Berlioz Requiem. Yes, however painful life can be, music transmutes it into calm beauty. Only music!

And that makes me think of Jennifer, Jenny, the Second Cellist, my Schubert companion. Who will often have to play in total unity with me. Since she emailed me, I've been thinking of her as being in a lonely, maybe frightening, situation, in crime-ridden Hamilton, in the basement of an empty house near the University (we have given quite a few concerts in the Great Hall there, over the years) and that she could come and live here! – and practice playing in total unity – In fact, occurs to me that this old house is big enough to accommodate all six of us – I must ask Alice about that, and whether we have enough beds & bedclothes etc (I could sleep at night in my wheelchair, or in an arm-chair, I've done that before – & if we worked out schedules etc – & then we could practise the Quintet, and play quartets – surely that will work?) – And *perform* the Quintet, as I have always longed to do! Listen together to glorious music – which would be a fine way of living through this period of enforced isolation, yes –

Who was it, which Classical story, where they all gathered together – yes, during a Plague – escaping the Plague – & told each other stories – *Decameron? Why* can't I remember? My memory – NOT Boccherini, I have played his cello sonatas, & I think a cello concerto, eighteenth-century composer – NOT Botticelli, medieval Italian artist, if I remember correctly – but – NOW I have it, BOCCACCIO, they take refuge from the Black Death & pass the time telling stories, in Florence – yes, that's it –

But, speaking of favourite music, I've been listening to one of my old CDs (talking of quartets) which I always used to play on Good Friday – Haydn's set of "Crucifixion" Quartets, glorious music – & now I think I'll listen to the Berlioz Requiem – but haven't I already said that –?

Should I first record the day's news about the Virus? Well, maybe it will have some value for the Future, if there is one. Is that why I'm doing this? And recording our chats. For Posterity. So here goes. The latest official count of Canadian cases, 18,000; number of Canadians infected, 2 million; prediction of 23,000-to-32,000 cases of infection by mid-April, with 500 to 700 deaths; present job-loss in Ontario, 400,000. And the concern about murderous Plague infections in old-age homes is now joined by concern about the vulnerability of prisoners in jails – Will there be good social changes when this society gets back to normal, if it ever does? It seems doubtful – but maybe I'm just a habitual cynic. Yes, Alice, I am!

I have been thinking about past experiences – as far back as I can remember! Happy & painful memories. Mostly painful. Well, the War – But then music, to the rescue?

Saturday 11th April
ANNA

A call from Jennifer quite early this morning (I think we're probably all getting lazy, staying in bed longer than before – or maybe it's just me getting old and making excuses!). Anyway, after friendly enquiries – I think she is concerned about my ability to shop etc, but she needn't be, I'm still capable – she made what seemed to be a silly offer – that I should live with her in her flat – and I thought Why should she suggest that, when I'm living not far from her in a house that's too big for me, opposite the Park and close to the supermarket? – and then I realized she was actually meaning something different, that she's lonely and maybe scared, as so many people seem to be – and so half-suggesting or hoping that I would invite her to live with me while this Pandemic goes on. Yes, and maybe it would make sense in other ways, for companionship, and she could help with shopping etc, and I do have a spare bedroom! – and none of my family have visited for a good while. But I didn't say anything on those lines and in fact ended the conversation quite soon after that.

Also some questions arose in my mind as I began to think things out, while I was drinking coffee after breakfast. When and if everything goes back to normal, will my life go back to how it was? And even, would I want it to, because to be honest I do get lonely sometimes in this house; a bit like Boris, I used to think, and his house in TO is much bigger and older than mine. When I lived there, and of course I was much younger then, I used to find it demanding, keeping the house reasonably clean, while cooking for him and so on; and that almost became too much for me, with my teaching and studies, although I was much younger then of course; and that's why we had that row and I walked out; and Alice took my place, you could say, soon after, and then he married her. I should have detached myself completely after that, but then I still had my music, I *still* have my music and always will have – well, at least as long as the Lark Quartet survives, and my teaching; and also he eventually apologized; I think Alice made him do that, she and I are second-cousins – Oh, Anna! Stop this! Just stop it and think about that young woman, Jennifer, and what to do about her.

And the Coronavirus (COVID-19, I wish they'd stick to one name! why don't they?). It's beginning to take a toll on all of us, and our lives: warnings from local authorities of very big fines, even more than $500 I think, if you are in the company of more than one (related) person and if you are less than two yards from another person! something like that – it's getting crazy! Hard to remember all the figures of where it's at now, but I think about 100,000 global deaths, including 20,000 American, 10,000 in UK now, and it's beginning in Africa (where one must fear that the death total will be huge): so seems all this has a long way to go, with enormous suffering. But will it result in a significant reduction in the world's population? Other people must have wondered, like me, if the world's population will be much reduced ultimately? That's also an issue in relation to global-warming, or should be? Too many millions of us human-beings! The world shudders and recoils under us.

Enough for now. Thinking about that girl, though, makes me also think about the Schubert and other music. It would be lovely to be playing it right now, calming, glorious! And we could play together, she and I, violin and cello: Schubert, maybe some Haydn or Mozart or Beethoven – jolly old Haydn, he would be best!

Sunday 12th April – Easter Sunday!
JAMES

A bright breezy day! We may be incarcerated, but at least there are many activities to enjoy. I've just come back from a walk to the Park, & there, as well as on the way there and back, neighbours were exercising dogs and shouting greetings across the street to each other (wish I could have taken you with me, Pusska – but at least you have been able to relax subsequently on the back lawn under my surveillance!). And one beggar I know came right up to me & demanded money for his lunch – I quickly gave him some quarters & almost ran away! And there was a runner who waved as if I was a friend, but he didn't look familiar. I thought of Ken – as I often do! –

& wished he was here, living with me rather than swimming in & out of my life. Maybe I'm just getting old & couldn't any longer function in the gay life of Church & Jarvis – well, I know I couldn't – though of course that has changed too since the days & nights of my wild youth. So long ago! I don't even want to try any of that now. Maybe I'm ready to settle down at last! – as Mom predicted I would, eventually, though I have always resisted.

But why am I spending Easter Day arguing with myself? It's up to Ken. And he's ten years younger than me – so why should he feel the pinch of Time Passing, the way I am? And surely I've shown him how much I care for him? We have so much in common. (Beyond chamber-music, Schubert's Quintet! Maybe.) Or is that perhaps part of the problem for him? But enough, James – enough.

I always turn on my bedside radio when I wake up, & on Sundays there's Michael Enright's "Sunday Edition", which is often good value. It sure was good value this morning. (Oh I should first mention that our dear Queen has given another uplifting speech, a short one, urging love & kindness – & her controversial PM Boris Johnson has survived his bout of COVID-19 – these items just before, or was it after, the news that the UK coronavirus death-toll has now passed 1,000, with 9,000 infected – & we also learnt that in Canada the forecast is 23,000-to-32,000 cases, with 500-to-700 deaths, by mid-April, which is this week! Isn't it? And what else? Bill Gates, billionaire, is financing a search for a vaccine, "the only way forward", but it will likely be 18 months before it is available! And meanwhile? Better not to think about that? And a final item – today is the 200th birthday of Florence Nightingale!!! End of my little news-summary. And I think the end of my news-summarising altogether. Too depressing. And –

"Everybody knows"! (Leonard Cohen) – or should do, or can do – every news outlet provides "fake-news"? – CBC TV advertises, non-stop, its commitment to informing us of the very latest "COVID-19 developments". It will exhaust our capacity to know or care! And so the end of this lengthy parenthesis.)

Back to "Sunday Edition" & forward to Enright's first item. Coventry Cathedral, bombed almost to total destruction by the Luftwaffe on Easter Day, 1940, but now restored, has a female Canadian Organist! called Rachel ?Mahon, lively & authoritative in discussing Canadian organ music (Healey Willan being the big name – English composer of English church-music). I enjoyed her interview, lively & knowledgeable – wish there had been more clips of her performing – As a young man, I was addicted to the organ (as to Christianity) – A choirboy in Toronto &, I should recall, a scholar at an Anglican Church school now notorious for the homosexual proclivities of its Masters (Yes, Ken, I'm glad you asked – yes, how could I have escaped? – of course I was a pretty & especially helpless potential victim) – but music saved me! I learned how to play the organ, had already fallen in love with the organ as a small boy, in the church services we were forced to attend in the School Chapel – & I was drawn also to the Organist & choir-master, a charming elderly man. Fatherly. (I told you about my actual father, you remember, what a bully he was, etc). A friend of his, to whom he introduced me, was a middle-aged cellist who had achieved a reputation across Canada & beyond. Yes, unless you are more stupid than I think, Ken (& you're not!), you've guessed it. Who he was. My future unfolded. I was not destroyed. I think.

Enough for now. You know, I've been thinking Can't we use our emailing, not only to entertain & communicate with the other four, but also sight-read some quartets together & even rehearse the Schubert Quintet? I defer to your advanced technological know-how. But after my next email, I'll try to communicate with all the others apart from you & find out exactly what they think, & what's going on with them – Boris, Anna & Jenny – I guess we're all feeling apprehensive & bored & isolated.

But please reply to this one only to me – I didn't intend to, of course, but I *have* told you about myself in this email, things I wouldn't normally tell the others, & now I think it's your turn to be Confidential, Mr Viola, & let me into the darkest recesses of your being! After that, we'll both be completely open to the others. Right?

Monday 13th April
JENNY

Oh, oh, oh, oh. The CBC news this morning is still saturated with that Quebec nursing-home scandal. 31 deaths of Seniors (more than one for each day of this month!), in appalling circumstances of neglect – & of course it reflects a general situation, in seniors' homes across Canada, as Staff fall ill with COVID-19 & can't be replaced, & helpless seniors are left in isolation, with night-clothes & bed-clothes stinking-filthy. Oh, to think of that – & it does make me think of when Mum & Dad died, he had Alzheimer's & she had a bad fall when she was visiting him, before she was knocked down & killed – but at least they had good medical treatment, & things to do, & pleasant surroundings, & they were together in one room, & we could visit – & the Staff were kind, one even telephoned me to talk about them & suggest that I visit. But that was in England, a few years before I immigrated here. In all my hospital-volunteering, here in Ontario, when I was an undergraduate, and then in my brief abortive nursing career during the SARS epidemic, I never saw or heard of anything as bad as in that Report this morning.

Maybe I should see if I can volunteer or give some help in the Hospital. If I had moved in with Anna, she's in walking distance to the Hospital, as I am – she sounded really welcoming when she phoned & offered me accommodation, last night. She said she has a spare bedroom – I thanked her, it was really kind of her. But I had to tell her that Boris and his wife had also just kindly offered me accommodation, in Toronto, she emailed last night – & I told Anna I had tentatively accepted, though with all the restrictions on travelling etc I wasn't sure how I would get there, to Toronto & their house – I mean with luggage – & I don't know if the buses & trains are still running. (CBC radio news just announced that the PM is very concerned about the nursing-home situation. New rules have been announced. Thank goodness.)

Quite chilly again today! But I must get out for a walk after lunch. So, what do I have for lunch? Cheese & bread & milk!!! Go get it, Jennifer! The fridge almost empty. One way of slimming? Ha ha!

But what else do I have to say here? Maybe my worrying is not so much about the Coronovirus & being shut-in, & the boredom & loneliness & almost-fear (if Angela was still here, maybe we'd find a way of getting together, but they've all long gone home, & the University's shut down – I wonder what they're doing, to keep sane? I thought of emailing her, starting an email correspondence like the one we had before, but I didn't.) The silence & lack of movement are spooky (when did any vehicle last come along this street?). But the garbage was collected this morning – thank goodness I put it out (just in case – remembering that Easter Monday wasn't a local holiday here in the past). Some things don't change!

KEN

A bright sharp breezy morning! If only this incarceration could end! But a telephone call from Jimmyboy while I was breakfasting – unusual, he usually emails, but maybe the isolation is getting to him too! (Or he badly wants to keep our emails private!) Anyway, he wants to get together (and so do I, though of course I didn't say so!), but also he seems concerned about Boris's state of health (he has high blood-pressure, & of course, being confined in his wheelchair most of the time, he doesn't get much exercise. And, says James, he seems to be sinking into a deep depression (I know he's vulnerable – Anna mentioned that, when she was his sort-of-companion-housekeeper years ago, he would just go into silence for long periods and she would worry about him, but he had a doctor then who jollied him back into circulation). James said he spoke obsessively, in the telephone conversation, about the Schubert Quintet & that we should all five of us get together, *must* get together, to rehearse it, & even perform it for ourselves! A quaint idea, maybe, but James is taking it seriously. And apparently Boris even talked about us all – Anna, James, Jennifer & me – going to *live* in his house! To rehearse the Quintet, & hopefully a Haydn or Mozart or late-Beethoven quartet or two (like James, I really want to get to know those late-Beethovens).

Come to think of it, maybe it could work – the house is big enough, I remember that – he had me round for dinner was-it-two-years-ago, when my predecessor, I think called Trevor, suddenly got married to an Australian woman & had to be replaced in a hurry – Boris was my viola-teacher. That's when I met James & immediately thought Yes, yes, what a good opportunity!!! – we could be a duet, musically & personally! – & anyway what good fortune it was to find a place for me & my viola in such a successful, well-respected quartet – bloody good luck, & it meant I could continue working downtown (*they* wanted me too!), & maybe eventually buy this condo I'm renting – an ideal arrangement – & it *has* worked out well so far – Yes & a short holiday in Boris's place would be fun, especially if James & I can spend intimate nights together? – So, I said Yes, fine, if we can all manage to do it. Apparently that old housekeeper, can't remember her name, would do all the meals – & of course we would contribute to expenses – Sounds great! Just when we are all getting to the point of going crazy with this unending isolation – enforced now with huge fines, apparently! And soon we'll be legislated into wearing surgical-masks everywhere! Awful! – but could distract attention from my messy too-long hair?

What else? Oh, I was almost forgetting – about James's suggestion that we keep in regular contact by email – he has been keeping a sort of diary, as I guess I have been too (I wonder how many of us, here in what used to be TO's "gay village", have been forced into recording our lives – now they have been emptied of all interesting content!) – but if we retail our thoughts, now that actions are wanting, he says, we can all get to know & understand each other more intimately (not sure I do want that! But why not try it?). He also says we *should* be in intimate contact with each other, we members of an admired Quartet! Even more than we already are. (I think it's all Boris's idea, probably.) It would apparently deepen our sympathetic understanding of each other & "the great music we are privileged to play" (James says Boris said that & I think he really did say that!). Anyway, he is proposing to send us all a sort of introductory message. It will read (James said, & I don't think he was joking): "Dear Fellow Members of the Lark Quartet, I hope you are all keeping well & employing your idleness creatively! As a group of five friends who love music-making, I think we could find mutual cheer & encouragement in directly communicating to each other our thoughts & feelings, & above all playing great music together. Your friend & fellow-musician, James." I think that's more or less correct – but I'll soon be able to check, when his email arrives. Of course, if we do all gather in Boris's house, we'll be in close (too close?) contact anyway. But that intensive emailing could be a good preparation for concord? After all, I hardly know Jenny, the additional Cello, & it will be pleasant to get to know Anna better than has been possible in the few short conversations we've had. Maybe in the end this shut-down will make us better people, more patient & kind (or maybe not!) – as well as reducing pollution around the planet (Eric has sent me an email that features a short film about world-wide reduction of pollution, with liberating effects for wildlife as well as humans, brought to us by the Pandemic – maybe we can *hope* for that, anyway!).

But that reminds me to give a troubled account of news in the media today. First, the horrific state of old-age homes in Quebec & other parts of Canada, no doubt including Ontario, with Seniors suffering not only from COVID-19 but also from being abandoned to filth & death by fleeing Staff (shown as not only being poorly-paid but also terrified of dying themselves – surely governments will *have* to remedy this situation after the Pandemic is finally over? I think Seniors will demand that, the ones who survive). Second, the beginning of political dissension over preparations for, & conduct during, the Pandemic (after the remarkable unity up to now) – especially in the U.S. as the horrific Trump bellows his dishonesty, confusion & incompetence into Brilliant Achievement, or tries to – (surely he won't succeed in bullying & bamboozling his way to a second disastrous Presidency come September?). (There's actually growing concern that he'll declare himself President-for-Life!) And of course there's more, much more, but I'll leave that to posterity to consider, evaluate (of course *this* is not fake-generosity, just fake-news?). Oh, don't try to be clever, Ken. You're out of your depth! So – come, I need a private session with Madame Viola to restore sanity.

FOUR

Wednesday 15th April
ANNA

Gloriously brisk, sunny morning! I'm just back home after a short totter round the block: must keep this old body going! Of course rain is predicted, so the sun will be obscured by heavy clouds pouring in from the West by this afternoon (Spring is still trying to pull away from Winter!), and so one must respond to any opportunity to get some fresh air and exercise. There was no traffic at all; cars were parked all along the street as if it was Sunday, and I saw only one other person, a neighbour taking his dog for a walk (we shouted greetings across the street). Since Hercule died six years ago, I've had no pet – decided it would be too demanding now (dogs should have at least one good walk per day) and also likely more costly than I could afford in retirement (considering the prices that vets charge).

Now I must get on with cleaning the bathroom, and other chores (what will I have for supper? But before that, some light gardening; my daffodils are in flower – I always feel daffs epitomize Spring, in their brilliant yellow; and I'll have my usual short rest after lunch). But I must first record my response when, returned from my walk, I found the latest *Maclean's Magazine* in the mailbox, with some bills etc – bright yellow cover featuring these words: "CORONAVIRUS / HOW DOES THIS END? / A nation in lockdown. A population in peril. We really are in this together." Another harbinger of Spring? But unwelcome, at least to me: there's an air of near-panic around us, and that's negative, destructive. I'll read that "Special Report" later, but surely it can't help Canadians to deal positively with fears and concerns. We must be hopeful, optimistic, determined to make everything better than it was, yes – But here I go, "chattering again, Anna!" as Miss Honikman used to call out, shaming me. All that time ago.

What James has suggested sounds positive and helpful, not only for Boris (if he is descending into another depression), but for the Quintet as a whole, for all of us. James said it was Boris's idea and he was very insistent, so it would be sad to disappoint him – especially as he doesn't seem in a good space, getting very depressed, James said. Boris said there would be no difficulty accommodating us all, and Alice had said she could certainly get in enough food for us all. And it would be so good, so healthy, to be together and playing great music together! "Remember the C Major of this life!" James said.

I'll go on keeping this private diary: it's an old habit, after all, and harmless and also, I think, useful. It'll be easy to email a few words to the four of them each evening, rather than telephoning as I have been, and good to hear from them. So I'll do that, as long as it doesn't evolve into a time-consuming chore!

But let me just summarise the latest "Coronovirus News". Across the world, nearly 2 million COVID-19 infections so far, with about 125,000 deaths (25,000 in USA). There are over 27,000 cases of infection across Canada, 8,000 in Ontario, and a total of almost 1,000 deaths (just yesterday, a reported 75 deaths in Quebec, 43 in Ontario). There is great and growing concern about COVID-19 in Seniors' Nursing Homes, especially in Quebec. Staff are ill or exhausted, so Staffing shortages have become severe, and patients are seriously neglected, and often in isolated and hideously filthy conditions. Horrible! And there are other problems connected with "our nation in lockdown": women virtually imprisoned with their abusers, for instance. Such a distressing litany. Apart from all the reports of financial disaster. Why try to record it all here? But I do. Habit, I guess. It will be a relief, I think, to be in Toronto with the others: no doubt they will also be very troubled, but we'll all be troubled together, which won't be so painful. And we'll be making music!

Oh, a telephone call from Jennifer. She started chattering about this and that, but I could hear the worry, the tension, in her voice. So I told her about my plan, that we, she and I, should accept Boris's invitation – even if James and Ken don't, but I think they will, and anyway they are in Toronto and not far from Boris. I could hear the relief in her voice, and of course she was almost embarrassingly grateful. I said I'd go across in my car to collect her and her luggage in the evening ("Just a small suitcase is all I'll have" she said, so I asked her if she wasn't forgetting something. "Oh, what, my toothpaste?" she replied. "No," I said, "your Cello" and she laughed, "No, I tie it round my neck & drag it wherever I go". I think we'll get on all right, the two of us. I said we'd spend the night here and then drive to Toronto tomorrow morning

"And if we're stopped by the RCMP, you'll have to say you're my long-lost little sister" I said). She wondered if it is really all right for us to go to Boris's house and spend a week there with him and Alice, and of course James and Ken too. I said I'm sure that he would have checked that out, if necessary, as it's *his* house and *his* invitation. So that's settled. I'll telephone or send an email to the other four, especially Boris and his wife, to let them know. I also told her I had face-masks, if needed (found in a bathroom drawer: a remnant of my SARS nursing days, obviously).

And now what? Get on, Anna!

Thursday 16th April
JAMES

And what about Pusska, my very dear Pusska, loving companion? "Now that I'm old and feeble, will you discard me? Remember, dear Master, how you saved me from starvation, a painful death? How you lifted me to the warmth and safety of your brave breast, how you took me to your nest and gave me life-preserving milk –" No, I mustn't go on in this sentimental vein. Just to evade the veiled scrutiny of your milky old eyes. We have had eight or is it nine contented years together. Fairly contented. Rarely a sharp human word or sudden feline scratch. And now – But first I'll have to find out how to do it. How to arrange your death, my dear. Because you were a foundling of mature years, I simply assumed that all arrangements relating to your physical state had been made prior to our connection. But now – How could I take you to Boris's, & for all I know he may have acquired a pet, dog or cat, since I was last there – and even then, any pet would probably not have been evident, in his lounge, as I remember he called it, or dining-room. Oh well – maybe I shouldn't go. Of course, if I say I can't, Boris will ask why – & my absence would be a problem for him and the others. I am irreplaceable as First Violin!

Well. I'll pray for inspiration. Maybe one of my neighbours could be persuaded to look after Pusska, or come in to feed him every evening – yes, surely that would work – but oh, I forget Social Distancing etcetera. Actually, on the CBC radio news this morning, & in our local newspaper, intimations of change, even rebellion – people, *some* people, are now questioning the need for social-distancing, for instance. But the bad news continues generally: in yesterday's paper, "Canada's COVID-19 death toll passes 900; economy could shrink 6.2% this year." "27,000 confirmed & presumptive incidents of coronavirus disease" – & in today's paper, over 1,000 of these fatal. On the other hand, Ontario's wildlife is predicted to "experience a population boom" – hear that, Pusska? Maybe, if this or a succeeding Coronavirus takes hold, humans will be wiped off the face of the planet, freeing the rest of "God's Creation" to proliferate & prevail? Stuff for a scifi novel that is surely being written right now! And I should also record that more than half of the Canadian COVID deaths have occurred, often in scandalously horrific circumstances, in long-term-care homes – this should, *must,* force governments to bring about reforms in the health-care of seniors. Jenny will know all about that.

Meanwhile there seems to be growing impatience over the "shut-down of the economy", especially in Trump's USA. And increasing international controversy about how information about the Coronavirus was handled, both by China (accused of deliberately delaying dissemination of information – when it actually began there!) & various Western countries (slowed by bureaucracy, hesitancy, lack of adequate preparation – by democracy itself?).

Oh, what else? I should contact Ken for a chat tonight, about arrangements for transferring ourselves to Boris's place on Saturday (assuming that Anna & Jennifer have both responded positively to his invitation – Anna did, last night & maybe they are already there, at Boris's place, or will be, by the time we arrive. It's not far – we'll go there in my vehicle, I assume (as Ken doesn't have one – I've always been troubled by his reliance on cycling or walking, in Winter especially – carrying his viola on his back! – & of course we'll need some more luggage, for clothes etc – as well as our instruments). I'll also take my laptop, so I can keep in touch with my extensive cohort of friends! They constantly need my affectionate attention!!! And Alice said Boris expected that we'll all have our iphones with us.

So that's IT for now, Pusska. I'd better call Ed about feeding & entertaining you in my absence (good that I stocked up on cat-food several weeks ago, the only variety of it you will deign to eat – because everyone was then talking wildly about Shortages – of toilet-paper especially!).

Friday 17th April
BORIS

Lark News, Volume One, Number One!
From Allegro House, Toronto

Here we go, my dear Colleagues and Lovers of Chamber Music: This is the Newsletter you have been awaiting! In this perilous time, it will provide you with the latest news and views about the Classical Chamber Music we admire

and seek to perform at the highest level we can possibly achieve, especially in the present challenging and troubling time when COVID-19 controls our daily lives.

Some of you will remember the series of lunch-hour concerts we have presented at Masterson University over many years – a quarter-century, in fact! During that period the Lark Quartet has changed in its membership, but three of us have been members since the very first concert: the Founder and Cellist, and the First and Second Violins. We're still here!

The Concert that would have celebrated our quarter-century, with our first performance of Schubert's great C-major Quintet (the masterpiece which crowned his short life of glorious creativity), has had to be postponed, like so many artistic endeavors, because of the Covid-19 Crisis; but we hope you will come to our concert on June 15th, which will include quartets by Haydn and Mozart, and celebrate the glory of Summer as well as express our joy and thanksgiving at the end of the Pandemic.

And so on! Alice and I composed this Introduction together. What do you think? If you all agree, we shall share the honour and responsibility of being Guest Editor of this new and exciting journal, which will preserve the memory of our imminent performance of Schubert's noble masterpiece in whose shadow we are assembling, and will also point to a happier future! (As you all probably know, I have long hoped that we would perform the great Quintet! What joy you are giving me!)

Please feel welcome to our humble abode! As you know, I am no longer capable of functioning on Toronto streets and in Toronto stores – this wheel-chair is difficult to move around, even in our home, and without Alice I'm sure I could not survive – I would starve! – so, thank you, dear Alice – you are another of those we honour and thank for your kindness and generosity! Like all doctors and nurses – those evening street-serenades of gratitude that we see and hear on TV are so well deserved!

Writing this, I know that Anna and Jenny will arrive soon and with Alice's help will settle into their room – which I hope is comfortable for you two! I hope you will have a safe journey – I believe even the Queen Elizabeth Way is almost deserted! Alice said the mattresses might be a bit too firm, but when we were sleeping there I thought they were fine – so, as I say, I trust you will be comfortable! James and Ken, you will arrive tomorrow – and you'll be in the two guest-rooms – and we hope you'll find *your* beds comfortable! Alice has been busy digging out sheets and blankets, she says – from what we used to call "kists" when I was briefly in Cape Town as a boy, after our escape from Nazi Germany just before the War, and before we came to Canada – I can't recall what they're called here, chests? My parents had one in their first store in Toronto, soon after we immigrated, I remember frightening myself by imagining that I had hidden in it and locked myself in – Yes, "kist" – Looking for words, and not finding them, has become a major irritant of my old age!

By the way, I meant to ask this earlier – please don't park behind our vehicle! Alice will need to use it for shopping, which is why it's parked there – but, for your vehicles, there's space for both of them in the Garage – as you'll see when you drive round our car. Sorry to be so – what? Obsessive? Usually I'm only obsessive in the way you know very well – Mind that F♯! don't forget that diminuendo! the quaver is important! *Every note counts!* & so on & on!

The news on the CBC this morning was troubling. In Ontario, 564 new cases of the virus, and in Canada as a whole, 30,000 cases now. 170 military personnel are on their way to help in the Quebec long-term-care homes where Staff are ill or have just not returned to work – a dire situation! I hope I've remembered the facts correctly. The situation is obviously serious, though apparently there is hope now that the total number of infections is lessening. Meanwhile, in the US there are cases of right-wing rebellion – people openly defying limitations on being close together, that sort of thing. I know the isolation of young people is becoming less endurable to them, but one hopes they will go on recognizing how important it is, the physical-distancing, for the sake of all of us. (Especially Seniors!)

Enough! You probably know better than I do what is happening! I have been thinking more about Schubert – and especially listening again to that recording I sent all of you, as our starting-point. I'm looking forward so much to having my cello between my knees and playing that glorious music – for too long that's been absent from my life! And I've been thinking – Maybe I should tell you, otherwise you might be hurt or angry with me, that in the last four days I have been informed of the death of a close colleague from my University days, and the death of one of my oldest friends – Death seems to be all around us – but Life will prevail!

So – Onward!

Saturday 18th April
JENNY

Yes, well here we are! Actually it was an easy journey, not many vehicles on the highway, or pedestrians on the pavement, in the City & especially here in Forest Hill. Anna drives carefully – ultra-carefully, actually, & of course she knows her way well, as she once lived in Toronto, & actually in this house!

It's a gloriously sunny breezy day, an English sort of day, I was thinking. And Alice was so welcoming! I liked her immediately, you can tell she is honest & straight-forward – & a hard worker, she obviously had to do a lot of preparation on her own – Boris couldn't help, even if he'd wanted to, & I'm not sure he would have! So she helped us carry our things into the house & up the stairs to this room – which is big & just a little shabby, this would have been the master-bedroom, until he had to have a wheel-chair, & then I suppose he started living in the big dining-room & his study downstairs – I wonder where Alice sleeps, probably on the chesterfield, to be close in case he needs help.

But enough of this – I'm just going to write down important things, won't have time probably to keep a detailed diary like I used to do! Good!

However, continuing bad news on the Covid front. Not a surprise! But disappointing that so many people, mainly young people of course, are so extremely fed up with being house-bound that they are starting to go back to their old ways – & that could be disastrous, returning us to "a high incidence of Covid infections", just when they seemed to be levelling-off. What will our authorities do to restore control, without losing public respect? And, talking of public respect, the second problem is of course the suffering & deaths of elderly men & women in Long-term-care Homes – agonizing for families & friends, who have found their loved-ones suffering in filth & despair. It's a huge problem of neglect, over many years, that will require a lot of work & money & political will to remedy. Family-members are clearly upset & angry. So, major problems – & at a time when, after Covid is brought under control, public finance will be so diminished by all the financial help that the Federal & Provincial Governments have been increasingly providing.

And the Covid figures announced today (I heard this on the CBC News, while Anna was driving us along the QEW, which was very quiet) – well, I hope I'm remembering this accurately – Over 500 deaths, 85 new cases today, & 10,000 cases altogether in Ontario (can that really be right?). Then there was a whole programme about the treatment (mistreatment?) of Seniors in the long-term-care systems, all of them under the control of Provincial Governments – health-care workers are demanding those governments urgently take control of all long-term-care homes, & reform the whole system – but will that happen? Anna didn't think it so, she was very skeptical, she said it all made her angry and she told me some of her experiences as a young trainee-nurse during the SARS Epidemic – even the doctors (*especially* the doctors, she said) refused to wash their hands! Said they didn't have time!

Well, that's enough. I must go to bed. Anna is still with Boris, I think they're planning rehearsals, probably also talking about the past! The mattress looks a bit lumpy but it's probably all right – I'm so sleepy, anyway. I think we were all a bit constrained at Supper, that's what Alice called it, and James & Ken were tense & didn't say much – they had arrived a few hours after us, & I think they're not too happy about being in separate rooms – that's if they're gay lovers, as I guess they are, but I may be wrong. I'm not an expert! But they live quite near each other in what they called 'the gay village' – which, they were saying, had changed a lot & I must visit it when that becomes possible! And all the time I was thinking 'But I won't be in the Quartet then!' of course – & if Boris doesn't think I'm good enough, when we rehearse the Schubert Quintet, I won't be in the Quintet either! But at least they have to put up with me here & now! And it will be an interesting experience, Jennifer! So to bed, to bed, & tomorrow to fresh fields.

Sunday 19th April
KEN

I slept in! Which implies that the bed is quite comfortable. I wonder if James slept well? Of course he's a good twenty or so years older than me (I think – should ask him) & he's not in good condition – told me he doesn't work out, just relies on walking. Now we're separated for the week (he says Boris definitely wants us all to stay here till next Sunday evening – which is beginning to seem like a long time – & already I'm wondering how Pusska is, in his new quarters – which I hope he won't decide is his new home!). I've been thinking that it may be time to have a real talk with James – here there should be time for that, neither of us can run away (I admit I have mostly been the guilty one!), & Boris & Schubert are a perfect combo, I think, to keep us calm & focused. Worth a try, for both of us & maybe the rest of the Quartet too. Anyway, I should go down & join the others & see what's happening, if anything! The water wasn't very hot, so I decided not to shower (I'll ask that woman, Alice, is that her name, she seems to run the house, if it can be hotter?). James always has a cold shower, even in winter (brr!) – but I need the heat! I managed to shave & at least make myself look clean. I hope. So now –

I did listen to the CBC as I woke up, the News, on the bedside radio – can't recall the new COVID numbers, but they were bad, especially the number of deaths in old-age homes – & apparently there's an increasing feeling now (especially, I'd assume, among the young) that self-isolation & physical-distancing aren't really necessary any more – but the authorities say it's too early, & dangerous, to "return to normal" – so we'll see what happens. "Non-essential travel" is what we're told to avoid – I told Boris I had wondered if travelling here could be considered "essential" & he said "Of course". Then I asked him if joining his household, the four of us, could be considered legitimate – he shrugged & smiled & said "You're here. What's the problem? Don't you feel welcome? You're a member of the Lark family. Oh what Larks!" When we arrived, I looked to see if there was any sign that anyone in the other mansions, admittedly far apart, along the street, might be watching – no sign of that, no movement, so I guess he was right. Apparently, too, stunt-driving & street-racing is happening now, along empty streets. But I wonder if we were just fortunate yesterday, driving across to here, not to be stopped & questioned by police? Were we disobeying any actual regulation? I hope not – just left that to James to decide, as he was driver & it's his vehicle. Guess COVID-19 doesn't need our help to prevail.

STOP this, Ken! No sound of movement, but GET DOWNSTAIRS & see if "Breakfast is Served"! If Jimmyboy has beaten me to it, he'll smile that superior smile (I wonder if he knows it infuriates me?). Maybe it's a good thing that we're separated – though it didn't seem that at first, especially with Anna & Jenny being together. (Suddenly occurred to me – does James wonder if, because of my disappearing act, I may have contracted the Virus? Surely not. But if so, surely he'd be glad we're in separate rooms?)

I guess I must look like a servant. That woman who presided over breakfast asked me if she could dictate the second LARK NEWS to me – is she Boris's wife, or secretary? Apparently she has "problems with the computer" (don't we all?) – Boris has told her to do that, & then through the rest of the week, each member of the Quintet will be required to contribute one of the daily items. What a bully he is – BAAS BORIS!!!! Another Trump. But maybe only that type of man could create & control a Quartet! So we allow him to scan our most intimate thoughts & news – why? Maybe because we assume he doesn't have the patience to be concerned about anything other than his personal ambitions & interests & concerns. And music. (Am I being sarcastic again? James accuses me of that. "Musicians are such egotists" he says – "Except me. I'm exceptional.") Anyway, I'll go find Alice now & she can deliver wisdom for me to send forth (separately from this diary-entry of course!) (Am I beginning to talk to myself? Or am I merely very tense in this wealthy-but-shabby house?) Madam, your obsequious secretary is ready. Dictate away!

LARK NEWS & VIEWS
Volume One, Number Two

I think you all know that Schubert's String Quintet in C Major was composed near the end of his life. After it, he composed only the three final Piano Sonatas and (of course!) some songs. He was born in 1797 and died in 1828, aged only thirty-one. He had lived all his life in Vienna, mostly in poverty. By the time he composed the Quintet, he had composed six symphonies (I have always loved the "Unfinished Symphony"!), an almost countless number of

glorious songs, and many admired chamber-works. You know all this. (Boris says I married him because of our mutual love of Schubert, and I say No, just for himself, that's more than enough, and he always replied "No, because of that Quintet, and we'll perform it one day, before I die!" So now we are all here, the Quartet he started half a century ago, and the plan is for rehearsing and performing a movement every day of this week, and then put them together for a complete performance next Saturday!

Of course, when we planned a performance of Schubert's Quintet, we didn't know that COVID-19 would be so very destructive, that so many people would lose jobs and income, and that most stores and facilities would be closed – and, as you know, we had to cancel all the Lark concerts we had planned and even advertised. You know all this, but Boris said "We mustn't give in, we must stand firm" and I know you agree, love and music conquer all. So here we are, and welcome to our home! As Boris says, "Music will always prevail", I'm sure you've heard him say that. Thank you!

FIVE

What? When? Where? Who? Why?
And what is our failure here but a triumph's evidence
For the fullness of the days? Have we withered or agonized?
Why else was the pause prolonged but that singing might issue thence?
Why rushed the discords in but that harmony should be prized?

Sorrow is hard to bear, and doubt is slow to clear,
Each sufferer says his say, his scheme of the weal and woe:
But God has a few of us whom he whispers in the ear;
The rest may reason and welcome: 'tis we musicians know.

(From "Abt Vogler", by Robert Browning – Boris's favourite poem; he declaimed passages from it soon after I met him, and then often later to me and anyone nearby; he seemed to know it by heart – a very long poem – I used to joke that it represented all he knew of English Literature, including Shakespeare!)

ANNA — And now, as penance for my somehow losing the email record of all the Quartet messages during the week when we rehearsed the Quintet for our Concert on Saturday 25th April, I shall draw on my defective memory to compensate for that loss. This will be my apology and tribute to Boris. All I can offer now! Here goes:

(Oh, first one comment about the circumstances. As we all know, our country, like most countries, is afflicted by the coronavirus COVID-19; and this mysterious disease, for which there is currently no cure, dominates our lives. Unless a cure is miraculously found, that situation may continue for an unpredictable period, maybe many years. So we must get used to it! But there is surely no need to despair! I am not clever enough to offer wisdom – but I will say that Music and Poetry offer relief and inspiration. Our Concert was surely inspired! Our Quartet – Boris's Quartet – may not survive, but its legacy does, in our memories and music-making! The Pestilence of COVID-19 also continues, but surely it will not prevail, if we are determined and positive in our response to it. We must stop destroying the planet on which we live, we must work hard and constantly to prevent violence and warfare, we must create art, we must enjoy our brief lives and make life enjoyable for all humans and animals. We should, we must! That's what I think. And then we will hear it – "the C Major of this life".)

FINAL COMMENTS on Schubert's QUINTET in C Major (Recalling as much and as accurately what the five of us – Boris, James, Ken, Jennifer and I, Anna) wrote for Boris in the diary-entries he ordained.)

Schubert composed his Quintet in C Major during the summer of 1828. In a letter written on October 2nd that year, he referred to an imminent private rehearsal of the Quintet; but he was very ill by then, and died on November 19th 1828. So he probably never heard his Quintet, and it wasn't performed until 1850.

1. For the Comments written when we were rehearsing the Quintet, before our performance on Saturday 25th April 2020, the First Movement (*Allegro ma non troppo*) was allocated to James – a good choice as, being First Violin, he had to set pace and intensity. I remember Boris telling him, during our rehearsing that Monday, "Go for it! Let's go for it! Schubert wants us to take notice, that's why the First Movement is so forceful and abrupt, and you notice that the melody is in C Minor – just the first of many unusual keys and unexpected key-shifts – Schubert is famous for them." Later in the movement, the two cellos (Boris and Jennifer) play a sort of duet in the key of E♭ – one of the many unexpected key-shifts in this Movement – and also in the Quintet as a whole. The movement, as a whole, is exhilarating, I think, and there are glorious passages when the two cellos sing together, and the viola and cello have a conversation!

I remember James saying afterwards that he had not known how fine that Movement is – like me, he had always considered it as primarily an introduction to the marvellous Second Movement! James also commented, if I remember rightly, on the cello duet that Boris and Jennifer had played so beautifully – I could see that he was impressed by her confident reading of the score, and the way she partnered Boris so accurately (of course there were some lapses, for Boris to stop and require repeats, but he was generally satisfied – indeed, my impression was that he generally admired her playing). And the rest of us did our bit, of course.

2. Tuesday: Jennifer commented on the Second Movement (*Adagio*): I felt almost jealous that Boris had given that to her! How I have loved loved LOVED this glorious Slow Movement since I first heard it many years ago, as a girl of (I think) sixteen! And I have listened to it again (as performed on the CD recording that Boris gave each one of us) countless times. This is music so ethereal, so – well, I run out of superlatives; it is such a joy and privilege to hear it! To participate in creating it!

The movement, in E Major, is dominated by a long, flowing violin melody, an ecstatic dialogue between cellos and violin, with a *pizzicato* bass; and then there is a loud, restless middle section; before it finally returns to the serene E major theme. Of course, there's much more to it – but, really, one must listen and listen to it, and marvel at its calm endless beauty – or rather, one longs for it to be endless! But life, and the Quintet, must continue.

After the performance of this movement, Jennifer sat in quiet stillness for some minutes, but I noticed that Boris was in tears.

3. Wednesday: Third Movement (*Scherzo: Presto* and

Trio: Andante sostenuto). Ken's comments. He wrote only a short commentary.

"Imperious, demonic" he said. "I remember a critic writing that about this Scherzo. I think of it as cheerful, uninhibited music – a strong contrast with the preceding movement – *and* with the *Trio,* which in the totally unexpected key of D♭ is surprisingly gloomy, almost despairing. When the scherzo returns, it resumes the boisterous, enigmatic uncertainty of its first appearance."

4. The final Movement, *Allegretto.* Thursday: I remember Ken calling this Movement an "idealized Viennese dance"! Well, it is certainly a fine contrast to the Scherzo, but, as Ken said, it does not, cannot, clear away the sad grey clouds that have threatened to end all cheerfulness throughout the Movement.

I'm not suggesting (and I don't think Ken did) that the entire Quintet is sorrowful – no, it's not, but sorrow lurks and often intrudes, even though vigorous delight finally wins. Or – not quite! Yes, there is joy in this, the Quintet's concluding movement. BUT the joy is threatened by gloom – in other words, there is a full representation of both extremes, sorrow as well as happiness, in this glorious music, as it ends. Happiness wins, I think – but only just!

The final chord *is* C Major, but it is almost contradicted, Boris said, by a penultimate "Neapolitan second" that momentarily holds off the final, satisfying tonic chord. "Schubert questions his own optimistic C Major," Boris said, "even as he is concluding his greatest creation; for, as he knows, as we all know, life is not endlessly happy: it includes suffering, and it comes to an end". (Yes, like the suffering brought by COVID-19, but Schubert and Boris say that joy will return – will win in the end!)

SIX

ANNA

Disaster! I am trying to face my dreadful failure, before telling the others. So soon after Boris left us. They will be devastated, as I am devastated.

The performance of Schubert's Quintet – No audience, except for dear Alice, but it was glorious, unforgettable, it will always be unforgettable. And there we sat, next morning, in Boris's home, relaxed, weary and happy. The concert had been a moving tribute – oh, to Boris certainly, and the Quartet that he had founded and led for a quarter-century; and of course to Schubert and his great composition (which we had performed with precision and delight); and to the divine gift, the great joy, of music; and to the Creator (Robert Browning would add) who gave us that gift, to help us endure the anxious sadness inflicted by the Pandemic and the dreadful murders in Nova Scotia. Yes. That can never be taken from us, none of it; our intense emotions, our deep memories. But –

Maybe we sensed that all was not well. We were all there, sitting around the table – James, Ken, Jennifer and myself – eating cornflakes and toast, chatting desultorily. Weary but content, as I say.

But where was Boris? We had been expecting to hear his wheelchair approaching. Preceded by his loud voice. But – Silence.

Then Alice came quietly into the room and stood near the door, just stayed there, with tears running down her cheeks. James stood up, went round the table to her, and took her hand. I think we knew then, I think we already knew, that Boris was dead.

After a moment, Alice said hesitantly "It was what he wanted. He asked me to thank you all for coming, and for performing the Quintet with him, and to say this to you, 'My resting-place is found, / The C Major of this life: so, now I will try to sleep.' I hope I've remembered that right."

"Yes," James said quietly, "you have. Thank you." He put his arm around her, and they stood together.

And I hope *I* got it right, too. My memory is poor now, and getting worse all the time. But I think we were all still puzzled. Obviously his death had not been sudden, unexpected.

"It's what he wanted" Alice repeated. "He planned it, and asked me not to tell anyone. You know Canadian law allows that now, 'medically-assisted suicide' I think they call it, and he had cancer as well as heart-disease. His doctor came early this morning, as Boris had requested. Only she and I were there with him – when he passed – and she has made all arrangements. He told me he didn't want a burial service, or a memorial service. 'The Schubert Quintet was my memorial service.' That's what he said.

"He had made all the arrangements, with the doctor, for – his 'departure' is what he called it – and for his body to be cremated. He made me promise not to tell anyone beforehand, he didn't want any 'fuss', he said. I was unwilling, he could see that. But after a while, I agreed. I had to. He was so determined. He wouldn't rest until I agreed, and I could see of course that my reluctance was upsetting him even more, and causing him even more pain.' She drew a deep tremulous breath. 'His doctor came, she was with us. And they will come to take his body soon. So if you wish to say farewell, you should go in now.'

After a few moments, we went slowly into his bedroom,

and stood silently near him for a while. I think I was still almost paralysed by the shock, and struggling to focus my mind. I could only think "The C Major of this life" and "My resting-place is found." He certainly looked more composed than I would have expected – more relaxed, almost smiling, lying there on his back, with the blanket pulled up to his chin.

Jennifer took my hand as we left the room, and held it tight. James and Ken went ahead of us. Alice was already clearing away the remains of our breakfast.

After a few moments of uncertainty, Jennifer and I went out into the garden. The two men followed, and the four of us sat in tense silence at the picnic-table until Ken said, loudly, almost angrily, "Well, I'm going for a walk", and set off. James, after a moment of hesitation, followed him. Jennifer and I went back into the house to help Alice in the kitchen.

But I haven't told you about my subsequent sad discovery. Whatever the cause (I have to think it was almost certainly my ineptitude), a long segment of my computer record of the period (Monday 20th to Thursday 23rd of April) leading up to our performances (Friday 24th and Saturday 25th of April) disappeared. Did I delete it by mistake? Surely not! But I must have, otherwise how could it happen? Four days gone – just gone, utterly *gone!* Just as we will all be gone soon. – And commentaries on each day by James, Ken, Jennifer and myself. Our complete daily diary record, such as it was. I told Jennifer about this catastrophe, and she tried to recover what was lost; she knows much more than I do about computers; but it was indeed 'lost and gone forever'. Fortunately, the diary-entries (by me) for our final two days here (after the Performances on Friday and Saturday) have survived. Of course the others probably have a record of their comments on the

Quintet rehearsals, and our performance, but Jennifer said it would be a lot of trouble for them, and probably distressing, to read their comments again now; and anyway, did it matter, we all had to move on.

Jennifer could see how upset I was. She tried to comfort me, and when I said "What will I tell the others?" she said "Nothing. They won't ask. We're all having to deal with Boris's death and with our plans for the immediate future. Soon we'll be leaving, all except Alice, we should talk to her about her situation. And we all have to face issues about *our* future."

"Will you come and live with me?" I asked, to my own surprise.

"Oh, Anna. Thank you. Let's talk about that. You've been so good to me."

So I was left in continuing uncertainty. But I could see that she was mulling over the idea.

"It's about Ken" she said suddenly.

"Yes, I know."

"You *know*? Did he say anything to you? Surely he wouldn't – and he has to think about James, you must know they have been close for some time?"

"James knows too. Jennifer, we should talk, all four of us, while we're together here. If we all agree. I think James is upset and hurt, they've been together for at least two years – more or less, though James told me they're having some difficulties in their relationship. So he was very quick to notice that Ken was attracted to you, wanted to be with you, talk to you – he even spoke to me a bit about that. And when you went for those late-afternoon walks with Ken last week, after the Quintet rehearsals – "

"Keeping a couple of yards apart – ! Not very obviously romantic, but maybe, when we are all so tense because of the

COVID-19 situation – So many changes are coming, once this crisis is over – so many changes are already happening – we can see already that our lives will be very different – So. I think Ken and I were really just exploring our impressions of each other. I like him, I really like him, he's lively, he's fun – but I like him as a friend, and that's what I decided I'm going to tell him."

Well, I've tried to recall that conversation as accurately as I can. It clarified our relationship, Jennifer's and mine. She also told me, I forgot to say this, that Ken said James hoped, if the Quartet continues, maybe under another name, that she would take Boris's place as cellist. Really, it doesn't seem right to be thinking and talking about such things, so soon after Boris's death; but maybe we have all been thinking of the future, we must all have seen how old he was, and frail – even though we didn't know how sick he actually was.

This is what I wrote sometime earlier, on a loose page that I've just found:

When we started the week of rehearsing the Quintet, Boris asked me to take over from him as "Editor" of our diary-pieces – he said he'd been too busy with the rehearsals, and anyway hadn't had much time (or, I now think, desire) to read what we had been writing (at his request, of course!). He sounded as if he regretted, or half-regretted, the whole thing – but it was *his* idea, after all! (He told me at the beginning that it was a way for each of us to get to know the other Quintet members as well as possible. But in fact it was not a good way, or very practicable.) Now, I think he may have been exhausted as well as ill – much worse, physically and emotionally, than we realized; and maybe not thinking things out very clearly. Anyway, I agreed. Though when the whole record of that week, together with our thoughts about the four movements of the Quintet, suddenly disappeared on my laptop computer, I felt both guilty and very stupid. And I didn't dare tell him: it would have been just before the great Quintet performance! (It was like the occasion when I somehow lost a diamond ring inherited from my maternal grandmother – and never told my mother! And was always fearful that she would ask me why I never wore it!)

Friday 24th April
ANNA

What a glorious day! Sun shining cheerfully, breeze ruffling the daffodils in the garden; magnolias in flower, cherry-trees in blossom; lovely, lovely! After breakfast, we sat for a while – all of us – on the deck. In silence. Then Boris cleared his throat and announced the day's agenda (no consultation, of course!). The morning is ours! We are permitted to walk and talk! Alice will go to the Supermarket to stock up on vegs and fruit, for lunch today and for tomorrow. In the afternoon, we will play two favourite quartets which we have performed quite recently (of course he has all the parts here) – Haydn's "Emperor", No. 62, in C Major (which we have played often over the years, a great favourite! I think Boris identifies with the Emperor! The second movement, I remember, is a set of variations on the famous theme that became a national anthem and a hymn-tune, I think); and then Mozart's "Dissonance" quartet, KV 465, in C Major. Neither of them is challenging for us, and James was clearly disappointed that we won't be playing one of Beethoven's Last Quartets, as he had hoped – but he said nothing, probably recognizing that it wouldn't be possible to play one of those without considerable rehearsal. I thought that once again Boris's aversion to Beethoven was in play, and I wondered again about the cause – it's always been an issue with him (clearly James would agree with me, though he and I have never discussed this), and I think it has weakened our Quartet's reputation – occasionally a critic, here or abroad, has noticed the lack of Beethoven in our programmes and commented on that. Anyway, too late to debate it, and I know Boris would just swat any criticism away: he has always been Boss! And after all, he did found the Quartet.

Sunday 26th April
ANNA

The news, on the radio, is ever more distressing and disturbing. Further information has emerged about the Nova Scotia murders that has stunned this nation and provoked a cry of horror and sadness. Almost unbelievably, 22 people were murdered, not far from Truro (I was born and grew up near there, so I know the area well, although I haven't been back there for many years). The perpetrator was wearing an RCMP uniform and drove a vehicle made to look just like an RCMP cruiser, and the whole rampage seems to have been sparked by an argument between the gunman and his girlfriend (who managed to escape him and give crucial information to the police – but she too, like the relatives and friends of all the victims, will be tormented, I think, by memories of the slaughter for the rest of her life). All that happened, I think, just after, or maybe even during, our performance of the Schubert Quintet. Hearing more details about it this morning on the radio was of course very distressing. As a Maritimer, maybe I was more intensely affected than the others.

We watched and listened to the CBC TV News that evening in silence. Boris and Alice weren't there – he was no doubt exhausted, after our rehearsals and especially our performance of the Quintet, and maybe he was also in great pain. None of us commented then on the murders in Nova Scotia. I guess we were too exhausted, after our concert, and all the rehearsing before it. And what was there to say? What happened was beyond words. Sheer horror. I hardly dare to think about it still. It was, and is, the very opposite of our performance of Schubert's glorious music.

And then there is also the continuing account of the COVID-19 Corona Virus spreading and killing around the world. Here, in Canada, a total so far of about 45,000 cases, with 2,500 deaths; in Ontario alone, over 13,500 cases, 750 deaths. There's increasing tension over the 'lock-downs', though not (yet?) here as angry as in the US. And much discussion and concern about the likely long-term effects of the disease itself, on national economies and the lives of populations in so many countries around the world.

So we are now surrounded by sorrow and worry. Sometimes I wondered – and maybe the others did too, Should our performance go ahead? And that was *before* the murders in Nova Scotia – which, as I said, we learned about after our concert. Clearly Boris wanted us to go ahead – performing the Quintet was maybe, for him, the Last Rite?

After breakfast that morning (Saturday 25th April), Alice pushed him in his wheelchair out onto the deck, and we followed dutifully. It was cool but sunny, a glorious Spring morning. When we were all seated, Boris cleared his throat, indicating that he had something important to say. "I know we are all troubled by the news of suffering, in Canada and around the world. But we also know that there is triumphant good in our world. I am remembering one of the great poems about the endless conflict between good and evil. It is also a poem about the ultimate triumph of goodness over evil. And it is about the power of music. Yes, you will remember it, I have quoted it before, often, often – Robert Browning's 'Abt Vogler'. Let me recite some of the lines I have known so well for most of my life. 'There shall never be one lost good! What was, shall live as before; / The evil is null, is nought, is silence implying sound; / What was good shall be good … / On the earth the broken arcs; in the heaven, a perfect round.' Also 'Sorrow is hard to bear, and doubt is slow to clear, / Each sufferer says his say, his scheme of the weal and woe; / But God has a few of us whom he whispers in the ear; / The rest may reason and welcome: 'tis we musicians know.' Yes, Schubert, our beloved Musician, *he* knew. And yes, we musicians *do* know. And the poem ends, you may recall these words, I have often quoted them: '… I have dared and done, for my resting-place is found, / The C Major of this life: so, now I will try to sleep.' The Abbot Vogler's instrument was of course a church organ, but I think his thoughts and words apply very directly to us. Yes, we musicians know – When I read Browning's poem for the first time, I was a boy still struggling to deal with memories of the Holocaust – which destroyed all my relatives, apart from my parents. I was – But now, let us prepare for our concert, for the joy and privilege of performing, on our five instruments, what for me is one of the greatest works of music ever composed. We have rehearsed each movement, now we are ready to perform the whole Quintet. You have the rest of the morning to relax. Then, this afternoon – 'the C Major of this life'", and he gestured to Alice, who carefully pushed him indoors.

I should say that my rendition of Boris's speech is obviously unlikely to be totally accurate. However, I have heard him make that speech before, in its essentials – one essential being those passages from a poem he has long admired (I remember his recommending it to me soon after I met him, and that I read it then, for the first time, as a young woman – in about 1970, I think).

James, who would have been similarly imbued with the poem (he has known Boris almost as long as I have), smiled at me, then sat down beside me. Quietly he said "Yes, the C Major of this life. You noticed that the two quartets we performed yesterday -"

"– are in C Major. Yes, I did notice, one could hardly miss it. Of course it wasvery deliberate, surely?"

"Yes. Surely. But exactly what does that mean?"

Of course all this was not only before the Quintet concert but before we knew about the Nova Scotia massacre, which also makes me think of "Abt Vogler" – "The evil is null, is nought, is silence implying sound; / What was good shall be good, with, for evil, so much good more ..." (But is it, is it?)

And so, our performance. Really, it was extremely demanding to perform that programme – even if to no audience other than ourselves and Alice (who stood beside Boris and turned the pages for him). But we were inspired. I don't think we ever performed the Haydn and Mozart quartets better, on the Friday afternoon (24th April); and then Schubert's Quintet flowed gloriously the next afternoon (25th April). Were there errors, deficiencies, in our performance? Oh yes, yes – "But God has a few of us whom he whispers in the ear; / The rest may reason and welcome; 'tis we musicians know." And I think we all *did* know. Afterwards, after the beautiful melodies, after those final questing chords, when the last echoes died away, we sat for how many minutes, maybe ten minutes, exhausted.

Then, a loud clapping. By Boris. Who was also weeping, sobbing. Alice helped him from his chair to his wheelchair, and pushed him in silence from the room. And the rest of us sat on for a while, in silence.

And the next morning (Sunday 19th April), news of the murders in Nova Scotia. But, while we were sitting there with our brunch of coffees and toast, a further shock was about to strike us. James had just turned off the radio. "Do we want to hear any more? Horrible!" "I wonder where Boris and Alice are" I said. "Probably still asleep, exhausted" James said. And maybe I was thinking "He's an old man, after all, and sick – was it all too demanding for him?"

Then Alice came into the room slowly. She said "Boris" and began to weep. "Here, sit down, Alice" James said, and helped her to a chair. "What's happened, are you all right, is Boris all right?" And she whispered "He's dead."

After sipping some coffee that I put in front of her, she began a hesitant explanation. I had assumed – knowing his health had been weakening – that he might have suffered a heart-attack during the night. But that was wrong. As Alice explained eventually, his death had been organized for some months, with the acceptance of his doctor (who arrived within the hour, accompanied by a nurse, and who dismissed us while she organized the removal of Boris's body). James asked tentatively about saying Farewell, and Alice, leaning on him, went with him into the bedroom. The rest of us followed slowly.

Then we went outside into the garden – Jennifer, Ken and myself – and sat there in silence. When James joined us, he said quietly to me that we should look after Alice. But Alice didn't need looking after by then. She told us that Boris had planned his death months before. Because he had not only a weak heart but cancer in its late stages, and could not live much longer, his wish had been officially approved, under the new legislation.

"I don't really understand why he was so secretive" James said. "And now I can see that he was actually challenging us to guess what he was up to. 'The C Major of this life' – two quartets in C Major, and, above all, our performance of Schubert's Quintet, a work that he said he'd loved and admired throughout his life, and had longed to perform, and now, finally – All of this adding up to an announcement of his intention. I hope he has found joy on the other side."

(Have I repeated myself? I think so. And there's probably some confusion in this account, especially around Boris's death and its aftermath. I apologise to anyone reading this text for any confusion (which is an indication of incipient Alzheimer's, no doubt – as well as grief). My life is changing, our lives are changing.)

And that's IT. Finished? A story of our lives – or, rather, a few recent fragments of our broken and uncertain lives. No different, fundamentally, from other lives. And of course from all human life, all life on this planet, threatened now by COVID-19. What will happen? The latest Canadian COVID-19 numbers are 50,000 cases, 3,000 deaths – and the Government's financial deficit to this point is $250 billion. How long will it take for Canada and Canadians to recover, when COVID-19 ends? Will we ever recover? And meanwhile, what of this polluted planet?

(When did I write that?)

ANNA

My final entry! I'll be glad to dispense with this "diary": it was Boris's idea, after all: an attempt, as far as he explained it, to make us all close friends, so as to achieve the best possible performances of the chamber-music he so admired; and ultimately of Schubert's Quintet. A noble Farewell. Did it work? I don't think so – if one notes the tension that increased among us, especially between James and Ken, but even between Boris himself and the rest of us. (I think he realized that, eventually.) Too much information! But maybe it also underlay the intense daily 'rehearsals' of each of the Quintet's four movements in that final week before our 'concert' (an audience of one, if you exclude the players: just dear Alice, whom I shall miss so much; more about that later!); but maybe, ironically, it also helped us all to become, again, miraculously, a unified musical 'machine': bad word; but what word could convey the living power of the music, together with our necessary collusion, our loving respectful determination to honour Boris, our Quartet, and above all, Schubert? Enough of that. " ... here is the finger of God .../ Existent behind all laws, that made them and, lo, they are!" Yes, enough, Anna! As Boris would have said to me – as he did once, actually, in one of his frequent critical comments during our early years, "You are so stupid, Anna!"

So, Jennifer and I will leave here after lunch, which Alice is preparing as I write. I suggested that she come with us to Hamilton, for a break – but of course that isn't really possible in present circumstances, as she immediately pointed out. "We will keep in touch by telephone" she said. Yes, Alice, I think we will, and she and I will be able to live together into our old age, if we both want that. I will talk to Jennifer about

65

the situation. She told me, when we started getting ready to leave, yesterday, that James had hinted she might take Boris's place as cellist, "if our Quartet continues" (but how can it, when Boris was not only the Founder but our absolute leader?). She is clearly restless, as I was at her age, when I was in thrall to Boris. And then there's her relationship, whatever it is or was, with Ken. Maybe, when the COVID-19 Plague is over, if it ever is, she will give up her Gerontology studies at university and decide to live in Toronto – as she once said she'd like to do? Or go West, where, I think she said, she has some relatives. So many uncertainties! And so many opportunities, at her age – or there should be.

Above all, there's the huge continuing problem of COVID-19! Just recently, with the Schubert performance, and Boris's death, I have almost forgotten about that! Yet it continues, and maybe intensifies; and even as more and more communities in Canada and especially the United States (far from united about this!) are "opening up", whole populations are struggling impatiently to maintain rules about social separation and so on – and increasingly there is resistance and impatience, while Governments and their health authorities try to maintain appropriate, safe behaviour. How long can that situation go on? I fear that it will all end in disaster; but that may be the pessimism and weariness of old age!

It's now Friday 8th of May, and I will end here. Nothing much more to record. I never kept a diary earlier in my life, and have no wish to continue writing this. (Who would ever read it anyway? Would I?) Today, I learned from CBC Radio news as I awoke, is the 75th anniversary of VE Day, the day that the Second World War ended in Europe. We should never, never forget that! Of course the atom-bombing of Hiroshima and Nagasaki was still to come, and *they* should never be forgotten either – and only then would that War be fully over. But still, it was the beginning of a new beginning, VE Day, a New Dawn! Wasn't it? No, don't answer.

Anyway, I'll end with the latest COVID-19 information, incomplete as it may be. I imagine many in Canada try to follow, and remember, the latest facts and figures. Why? Well, we all need a general understanding of how we should behave, for the good of all, in the present conditions of our daily lives! (Though there may be surprises, even for Jennifer and me as we return to Hamilton this afternoon.) Anyway, here is the present state of the Coronovirus Plague. Yesterday, Thursday 7th May: Globally, over 250,000 COVID-19 deaths. Across Canada, over 60,000 cases of COVID-19 reported, and Canada's coronavirus death toll has passed 5,000, I think, more than 1,000 of those in long-term care institutions. In Ontario, 1,361 deaths in all. (Toronto alone, by the end of April, had recorded 5,550 cases, with 365 deaths – "shocking numbers" some medical authority commented.) But also "60-70% of Canadians support a slow easing of measures to control the spread of COVID-19". Notably more masks are being worn along the streets, apparently, and "social separation" (keeping 6 feet apart from other humans, in public places) is being generally maintained. More than 3 million Canadians have lost their jobs owing to COVID-19, and the total number of those now out-of-work is well over 5 million. Yes, a disaster, a disaster.

So what is our future? On this cool Spring day (Friday 8th May 2020), I look out at the garden: daffodils still in bloom, swaying bright yellow in the breeze; magnolias and cherry-trees in glorious pink blossom. "Joyous Spring" says Nature, poor wounded Nature. And our response? Do we have one?

Tuesday 12 May (I think) (A glorious sunny day!)
ANNA

James and Ken departed before Jennifer and I did. They were obviously stiff and cool with each other (and with Jennifer and me), but hopefully they would have relaxed during their short journey. James was very affectionate towards Alice, insisting on a 'get-together ASAP'. When I enquired (tactfully, I hope) about her longer-term future plans, Alice said she was 'thinking of turning the house into a residence for students and a few elderly women'; but hoped to accept my invitation to visit me in Hamilton as soon as possible. And then she suddenly started talking about Boris again. I was surprised, and just listened, mostly in silence. Not that I couldn't understand her emotions, thinking too that she will now be on her own, at least until the Pandemic lessens, and with nobody to talk to – well, nobody who would immediately understand. But also some of what she said was new to me. In our years together, Boris did not talk much about his past, for whatever reason – well, I do think he was inclined to look down on me as an immature female! He was a man of his generation; he didn't take women, especially young women, seriously.

Anyway, to summarise some of what she said. Recently, before the invitation to us for the Quintet concert, when he 'became obsessed with that', she said, Boris had talked more and more about his youthful years in Cape Town; he had enjoyed the warm climate, the sea-swimming and mountain-climbing, as any young boy would – especially after the constriction and fear of being Jewish in Hitler's Germany. But his Father had decided, when the War ended, to emigrate to Canada; he had learnt that some cousins who had survived the Holocaust were settled and prospering in Toronto, and he was also disturbed by what became known to us all in later years as Apartheid; in Cape Town there was a vigorous population of "Cape Coloureds", people of mixed race who lived in a crowded area called "District Six" – I don't know why I remember that when I can remember hardly any other names! Boris told her that he had loved the free-and-easy lifestyle, and had friends who taught him to enjoy music and dancing – did you know he was a great dancer in his youth? (No, Alice, I would never have guessed that!) In Canada, he was sent to a prominent boarding-school where he was beaten and abused: his Father had quickly become quite wealthy, as a partner in a prominent company established by relatives. Boris became rebellious, refused to join the company, and "travelled the world", he said, as a young man. Then he returned to Toronto, after his Father died unexpectedly, leaving him this house as well as, he said, "a small fortune"; so he was able to study and teach music for the rest of his life. "It's all I ever wanted" he told Alice. "Learning, teaching, enjoying the greatest music ever composed." Well, I wondered. But then, he had never given me what I knew he could have given – encouragement, gratitude. He had eventually been appointed to a research position at the University, and, Alice said, he became fascinated by Medieval literature, and at that time read and reread Boccaccio's *Decameron,* on which he had become a "recognized expert", giving lectures on it occasionally. About a group of young aristocratic Italians who flee Florence to escape the Plague, in the Middle Ages, and then entertain themselves in a rural retreat with story-telling and music.

Boris was our Pied Piper, you might say! And the Lark Quartet was his best-known creation, his greatest achievement. Now it's gone. Does that matter? Do any of us matter? Victims of this Pestilence, this Plague, this COVID Pandemic?

Jennifer and I set off after lunching with Alice. We thanked her for her hospitality; "You're very welcome" she said. Then we ate in near-silence. Exhausted?

There was much less traffic on the highway to Hamilton than I had expected. At first Jennifer and I continued our silence. Then I asked her what her plans were.

"Well, I guess to go back to reality, whatever that is" she said. "I don't know if the University will function at all for a while – even small classes won't be allowed, and it looks as if all educational facilities will continue to be locked down, at least until COVID-19 is clearly under control, and who knows how long that will be?"

"You know you'd be very welcome to live with me in my house" I said. "You'd be completely free to come and go, of course. We could work out a productive way of sharing shopping and the kitchen etcetera, and – well, I know we could work out everything amicably."

"Oh, Anna, that's so good of you. Yes, I'd like that. I know we could work things out without any problems, as you say. And I have to work out my *future* too – once things are generally a bit clearer. I do have some savings, but I know my Uncle can help if necessary, he said to just – I'll call him tonight. Did I tell you he lives in Vancouver? Or did. I thought of going to live there, but I guess that wouldn't be sensible or even possible as things are."

"No, I think you're right. I wonder what changes are coming? Did I tell you that I was worried the Police might come after us, at Boris's house? We weren't wearing masks, and I think that's maybe required now in public; when shopping, or even walking? I'm sure that you and the others kept the right distance apart when you were out walking near the house. But I was mostly worried about the five of us – six of us, counting Alice – in the house. I didn't think about that at first, and of course we couldn't possibly have spread any infection beyond the house, if we'd had any to spread, but I think it was still disobeying rules – Well, you get so worried about unintentionally disobeying rules of behavior in this sort of situation; and being a cause of spreading that terrible virus? What do you think?"

"I must admit I didn't worry about any of that, but I'll have to now, won't I?"

And we arrived in Hamilton.

P.S. (five days later)

And so: Life, as they say, Goes On – But the effects of the COVID-19 Plague will certainly be profound, reducing populations and economies, and causing major changes in daily life and behavior around the world; mainly negative changes, surely; at least until things settle down? And worst of all, some think (and I agree) that COVID-19 has distracted attention so profoundly from the ever-advancing threat of Global Warming, the general degradation of the world, and the widespread destruction of wild-life, that the future, even when the Plague does end, seems bleak indeed. – So, Boris, what do you say now? "The C Major of this life"? No? G Minor? And I am glad that I will probably follow you into the Darkness before long – before the next Plague arrives.

Monday 18th May
ANNA

Gloomy morning! Light rain. Temperature (I think) about 11 degrees. We have decided to take a trip to the Butterfly Garden, on the edge of Dundas, and have a walk there before lunch. Somehow it has remained open while all other local parks and recreation-areas have been locked-down; but it seems that public Parks and maybe even camp-grounds may soon be open, by Ontario Govt decree. Our world is about to open up again – but with nervous concern about possible further outbreaks of "Covid" (as people are referring to it increasingly, I think: the past will be known as "Pre-Covid" and the future as "Post-Covid"?).

It's a holiday! VICTORIA DAY. I think Canada is the only country that still celebrates (with fireworks!) that sad monarch, who mourned the man she had adored, and lived on and on and on. But writing this reminds me to telephone dear Alice, for another bout of mutually-encouraging chat. Yes, as soon as I finish writing this Farewell!

Hard to know, or even guess, where we'll be (IF we'll be?) in even the near future: as Canadians, as North Americans, as human-beings. And will democracy survive? Unsatisfactory as it is, it's surely still "better than the alternative" (as Churchill claimed): better than a world cowed by aggressive nations ruled by rich bullies who, like Trump and fellow-autocrats, bash as "fake-news" any attempts at truth-telling, and who viciously exploit whole communities to increase their personal power and wealth. And will we, can we, find ways to end the despoiling of this beautiful Earth, before it's too late? And – So many worries beyond the horizon of our Plague. But I am merely an elderly woman On Her Way Out! Who writes, who chatters, who Repeats Herself, who is totally without influence! Oh, Alice, dear Alice, where art thou?

Thursday 28th May
ANNA

Oh, a miserable day. Pouring rain. Grey, grey. Morning news: COVID-19 death-count in the United States of America: over 100,000: more than the total number of US deaths in Korea, Vietnam, etc. What about today's Canadian numbers? Do I really want to know? I have a vision of corpses piling up, piling up, as in those photos of Auschwitz that one struggles to forget.

But most immediately troubling news came in early-morning phone call from Ken. James in hospital with COVID and may not survive. "They won't let me see him, I begged them but –" Ken was crying, and now I am too. "I can't bear it" he said, over and over.

You can, Ken. You will, Ken. You must, Ken.

ADVENT

ONE

Anna: Sunday 8th November 2020

Dear Jennifer and Ken,

Another lovely day! Like yesterday, the day you two left. I am already missing you so much, dear Jennifer! But I promised not to trouble you and Ken, on your long drive from Hamilton to Vancouver. So I'll wait a few days before I write again, and of course I won't expect any detailed news from you until after you've arrived and met your Uncle and settled in there. You know, I hope, how much I'll be missing you! I telephoned Alice last night (she sends her love to you both), and mostly I'll be sharing your and my messages with her; like this one. (I guess Boris got us used to sharing our emails with everybody!) Alice and I both hope of course that you're having a safe and pleasant journey, dear Jennifer – and you know that we'll both be missing both of you so much!

It's another lovely day here: cool but dry and sunny. Yesterday was like this too. And it's been such a fine Autumn, and Winter still seems far off. *Fall* – I've always loved Fall! And I think most of the leaves have Fallen now! – all those glorious yellow leaves, and especially the red leaves. Down now and making a mess on paths and sidewalks and streets! But we did appreciate them, didn't we – not only as themselves but also because they cheered us up during this horrible Pandemic. We have to wear those masks here now, as you well know, and socially-distance, near any strangers – shopping and so on – but as my favourite poet wrote, "For all that, Nature is never spent" – I hope I've quoted that correctly!

But you must know the great news: what happened later yesterday, on the day you left. Biden and Kamala Harris defeated Trump! We agreed that it will take a good while for the U.S. to get back to anything like normal after the four ruinous Trump years. But will he go speedily or maybe at all? Not likely. And then what happens? Poor Biden, having to clear up that mess – and deal with COVID, which seems to be out of control in most of the States, and so many Seniors dying. And, like here in Canada, the economy falling apart. Huge problems! But I won't go on – sorry; you know all about it, I'm sure, and are just as relieved as I am to know that the Trump era should soon be over.

Anna: Wednesday 11th November
Dear Jennifer and Ken,

Here I am again! No message from you, but I expect you're fully occupied driving such a long distance, and then needing a good sleep every night. So I won't nag! Alice and I will just go on hoping that the journey is going well for you, and we look forward to hearing from you when you get a chance.

Of course you know what today is! Remembrance Day. The ceremonies have been cut back, and in London they say that only a few people were invited, with the Queen (wearing a black mask) laying a wreath at the Cenotaph. In the past, I have always attended the one in downtown Hamilton. I may have told you that my Uncle Donald was killed in the Second World War; my Mother's favourite Brother, and she told me once she had hoped to have several children and at least one son; but she only got me!

I won't go on, when you probably have so much to think about. I hope your journey is safe and pleasant. I look forward to hearing about it; in time, later, I mean! Look after your-selves! The only other news of any importance is familiar to you: more and more COVID deaths, and much worry and even confusion about schools and education; people are get-ting angry and upset with the politicians, but then the politi-cians have such difficult decisions, and can't please everyone!

Anna: Wednesday 11th November
Dear Alice,

I'm just sending you a copy of my email to Jennifer and Ken. I'll telephone you this evening, it's always lovely to hear your voice and have a chatter – you said you like having cop-ies of the emails that I send Jennifer. I know you're like me: very concerned that they stay safe and are happy.

I don't think I told you what a surprise it was when Jen-nifer told me she thought she was in love with Ken. You know, I'm sure, that they talked a lot to each other at your and Boris's house, and especially when they went for (social-ly-distanced!) walks together, during that week when we were rehearsing the Schubert Quintet. But she told me when we left your house to return to Hamilton that any love between them would be impossible: there was James to consider, and any-way she wasn't *sure* about her love for Ken, she said. Of course they couldn't be together at all afterwards, Jennifer and Ken, living in different cities; but I know they talked together often, long telephone conversations, especially after James died in July. I asked her again if she was *sure* that they were in love, and she said Yes, Yes, Yes. And then the next thing, she said her Uncle in British Columbia had invited them to visit, apparently he has a big house, and Ken was in favour of go-ing; and he would do most of the driving (I knew that she has her licence, from a few years back, but I was surprised that

Ken could drive because he told me he always rode his bicycle around Toronto, he feels strongly about global-warming; but now he said that James had left him all his possessions, didn't want his family to have any of them, they had always been ashamed of him because he was gay, he said; and so Ken inherited the car!).

Well, that was a long story – sorry! I thought I should tell you it all, privately. It's easier in a way to *write* something like that. But also I am getting worried – not *seriously* but enough to wonder if I should contact the Police – the R.C.M.P., I guess. Just in case Jennifer and Ken have a problem of some sort. Though that doesn't seem likely, and I know they would be embarrassed and upset, if there was no need for worry – as I think would probably be the case.

So, dear Alice, what do you think I should do? Probably unfair to ask you – but any *decision* would be mine, you wouldn't be to blame, they wouldn't even know I asked you.

Anna: Friday 13th November

Yes, it's *me* – Anna. But where are *you*, dear Jennifer? Alice and I have been wondering. Please contact me A.S.A.P. I imagine that you and Ken have reached British Columbia by now. Surely you have? Though I know of course that it's a very long way. I hope it wasn't too cold sleeping in your tent at night! If you did. Perhaps you are with your Uncle in Vancouver now. I hope so, and that you are both keeping well.

Alice and I are longing to hear from you! Are you having good weather? Here we are still having an unexpectedly warm spell (almost halfway through November!), but most of the foliage, the glorious canopies of red and yellow leaves that have delighted Alice and me so much, they have fallen now and lie like a carpet on paths, sidewalks and lawns. We both actually had breakfast and then tea on our decks this morning! And as Alice said, 'I think that's the last time 'til Spring, don't you?'

You might be surprised to know that Alice is going to join me here in Hamilton soon. I have just had a good telephone chat with her. After you left, I felt sad and tense, and when I telephoned a week or so ago, to tell her that you and Ken had decided to go West, to your cousin in B.C., she said she was still feeling like that too, sad and tense – not only because of Boris's death, which of course you will also remember so well, but also because her three university-student lodgers had gone back home to China as our COVID-19 infections were increasing here – so Alice was feeling quite lonely too. It's more than six months since Boris died, isn't it, but I think she is feeling sad and bereft, as I still do (I play the CD of the Schubert Quintet when I feel really 'down', as you know – and it gives me some comfort, especially that glorious slow movement). We need music! Or *I* do! You know that I play my violin quite often. Especially Bach's three Sonatas, which, as you'll remember, I *love*. Especially the third movement (Largo) of the Third (in C Major, of course!). And I try to concentrate on the music and not think of Boris and James.

I offered to drive across to Toronto to bring Alice here. She said Thank-you but she should give her own car some exercise! Then she said she might be able to come soon and stay for a couple of weeks, but now it seems that the Pandemic is getting worse again, not only in Canada (it's been very much worse in the United States all along, as you know – so many deaths). Where will it all end? Sometimes I wonder if it ever *will* all end, but I guess that's my pessimism showing, and I wouldn't say anything so depressing to anyone else. But they say that most Operations are again being put off, and

Hospitals are almost full with COVID patients, and medical staff are getting very close to exhaustion and collapse (I wonder if things are as bad in B.C.? I don't think so, according to the News). Also so many restaurants are going out of business now. Or *have* gone out of business. Oh, and of course, as you'll remember, most of the deaths have been of Seniors, in Seniors' Homes. I guess Alice and I are quite vulnerable! We'll have to be extra-careful. Most of us are used to wearing masks now – not yet when just walking along the street, or walking on the trails, but *always* when we shop.

Oh, Jennifer, I think I'm just telling you things you already know. I guess that's because it's all on my mind all the time now! On *all* our minds. I should be used to it, you'd think. But it's getting worse, and the latest is it seems that Christmas, which we have all been looking forward to – well, it won't exist this year, as a big family reunion occasion or with dinners and parties, it'll just be cancelled. Sometimes I think that Boris knew more than he thought he did when he decided to arrange his own death! (But I *shouldn't* think that: he was in great pain with cancer that we didn't know about.) And I try not to think too much about James – dear James – please don't mention this to Ken, I'm so glad Ken's with you.

Sorry, dear Jennifer, if I've been depressing you! Please don't worry about me. I'm one of the privileged ones – just as all of us are privileged compared to so many suffering in Africa and the Middle East without adequate medical facilities, doctors and nurses. But I'm looking forward so much to hearing from you! I guess you're too busy or preoccupied to look at your emails, and send me a reply. But you'll know I'm thinking of you, and Ken, and I send you my love.

Anna: Saturday 14th November

My dearest Jennifer,

Brilliantly sunny morning! I think I'll drive up the Dundas Valley to catch the very last of what has been a superb display of Fall foliage – surely we have never had such a glorious Autumn! BUT – oh, the COVID news is so troubling, and even frightening. As I always do, I turned on the CBC for the morning news. Since we know now that Biden will be the new American President, replacing, thank goodness, that immoral disgrace, Donald Trump, our headlines and discussion are now focusing back on the rapid increase of COVID infections and deaths in Ontario and many of the other Provinces, including now B.C. I think – with growing concern, almost panic, as Winter approaches; and one report was of a Hospital in the North barely able to cope! Confusing Official messages, here in Ontario, and growing fear, especially among older people (like Alice and me!) – for we are mostly confined in our homes, of course, or Seniors' Homes, with our fears and loneliness. Family and friends can't visit, as you know. I must make another attempt to persuade dear Alice to come here – and I *will* telephone her, this evening – or even join her in that big old house in Toronto if she insists on staying there, and invites me; though I know I'd probably be troublingly aware all the time of Boris's absence. I'll telephone her again tonight.

Meanwhile, Old Woman, get on! Yes, I *will* drive up the Valley. I need some change.

I'm back! 4pm and it's already dark (what a difference the time-change makes!). The radio forecast is for rain during the night and (I think) all tomorrow, with temperature close to freezing. I drove to Dundas and walked around the Butterfly Garden: no butterflies there now, of course (I hope the Monarchs are safely home after their long flight – which makes me remember that every Friday 13th motorbike gathering at Port Dover, I think. I hope they listened to warnings and cancelled it – and it also makes me think again about you and Ken, so please put me out of my misery, dear Jennifer, and email me!!!). It was good exercise, that walk, and I certainly did need the exercise. I'm getting so old and stiff and lazy! Now I'll have my supper and go to bed! What an exciting life this Old Woman leads!

Anna: Sunday 15th November
Dear Jennifer,

Still no email from you! And I had a dream last night – I very rarely dream now, so it was a compliment to you. You were smiling that radiant smile of yours, and then you hugged me. It was a lovely dream, even if it made me remember the last time you *did* hug me – which, you'll remember, was when you were about to leave, you and Ken – he was holding his car door open for you.

But our glorious Fall weather is gone now, and so is the sun, and it's raining. A DARK DISMAL DAY. What a strange thing the brain is! Why would an old rhyme get into my brain? – 'It's raining, it's pouring, the Old Man's snoring' – and who *is* the Old Man anyway? I don't think it ever occurred to me to ask that before now. And of course it's just nonsense anyway, and I'd better stop or you'll think I've gone round the bend! Maybe I have. I'd better have my shower and (as my Mother used to say) Get On! Before you left, and even before you came to stay, I would never have been doing this, emailing before breakfast in my nightgown – shows how I have Let Myself Go! (another of Mom's favourite sayings).

The only way I get news now, as you may remember, is

on the radio. I cancelled delivery of the newspaper when we went to Toronto for Boris's Quintet Occasion, and just never got round to renewing it. Anyway, I was going to say that I learned early this morning that this weekend is DIWALI (hope I've spelt that right), which is the Hindu and Sikh celebration like our Christmas, and of course it's a problem for them too – gathering together to worship. Especially now that the COVID infections are increasing so fast almost everywhere, and more and more people are dying of it. So it's hard to even think about celebration! There's a record high number of infections, and deaths, not only in countries like the U.S.A. and Mexico (in this morning's news) but in Canada, even in Provinces like Alberta that haven't been badly affected before now; and increasing warnings that medical staff and facilities are near breaking-point. Yet some people are still refusing, on principle, to take precautions, even wear masks. –

Oh, here I go again, being dreary. Sorry! But it's so much on all our minds. Maybe you and Ken are – well, not free of it, but enjoying new activities, and seeing new places and new people. Exploring Vancouver and its surroundings. I hope so, dear Jennifer. I do. Very much.

I am *so* looking forward to hearing from you! I hope you don't think I'm nagging – it's just that it's now ten days, isn't it, since you and Ken left, and I am missing you so much!

Anna: Monday 16th November
Dearest Alice – I assume that you have been getting the copies of my emails to Jennifer. This email I'm sending just to you – because I'm getting worried, but I don't want to worry *them* unnecessarily. She was always very dependable, and she promised that as soon as it was convenient (when they were well on the way, I thought she meant) she would email me.

Well, I waited deliberately but she hasn't, and I thought at first that just meant she and Ken – well, that they were preoccupied with the journey, or maybe each other, getting to know each other better, their decision to go West to the relative of hers that she mentioned, an Uncle in Vancouver who had invited her, and she badly wanted to meet him – did I tell you all this? Or maybe, I hope not, they've had problems on the road. I wish I had her Uncle's email address or telephone number, I should have thought of asking for it. I can't even remember his name now – she did mention it once, I think. It's over a week now since they left. If I don't hear soon, I'm thinking of contacting the Police – the R.C.M.P. What do you think? Am I getting worried unnecessarily? But it's a bad time to be travelling, I tried to tell them that, what with COVID and Winter coming – maybe I should have been more forceful –

Anyway, dear Alice – And have you decided when you'll come here? I'm looking forward to that very much. You don't need to bring anything except clothes, of course, and anything very personal you might need. Maybe we will be able to play some music together, in memory of Boris – you said, I remember, that Boris once taught you the cello, and of course Jennifer's cello is here. Or would that be upsetting, for both of us? Or you could play the piano and accompany me, as Jennifer did sometimes.

But maybe I should say more about Jennifer and her relationship with Ken? It started during that week when we were rehearsing the Schubert Quintet. Maybe you saw that. He and James were very close friends but had had some sort of quarrel, before they arrived, and then Ken and Jennifer began to get to know each other during that week, sitting and talking in the Garden and going on walks in the neighbourhood ("always social-distanced, of course," she told me, "so we had to shout at each other"!) She implied that it was frustrating; that she enjoyed his company, but – And it couldn't go any further afterwards, anyway, when he was back with James in Toronto and Jennifer was stuck with this Old Woman in Hamilton. Actually, she and I did get on well, and shared the cooking and housework, and we both carried on with some teaching or studying as long as possible. And reading, and playing or listening to music, in the evenings. But then James died of COVID in hospital, and their cat died too, and Ken fell into a deep depression – and he told me just before they left, that even just thinking of Jennifer had "saved him" at that time – "and I knew then we loved each other truly, deeply, and must always be together". So you see, it's a love-story, isn't it?

And you've probably heard enough now from This Old Woman, hey? (That's what Boris used to say sometimes, "Hey!" – from his South African boyhood, I think.) I'll be looking forward to your next telephone call, dear Alice. And to your arrival!!

Love – hey? – Anna

Anna: Tuesday 17th November

My dearest Jennifer,

Such a chilly grey day! And I must admit that I was very depressed this morning when I woke up, and heard on the CBC a series of very sad comments on our Current Situation – which is deteriorating fast, even as I write this – though I don't want to depress you, dear Jennifer, and Ken; and more cheerful news came when I listened to the CBC's midday news: that apparently two of the newly-created Vaccines have tested positively! Let's hope they will be available soon!

I hope that, wherever you are, all is going well for you. I am longing to hear from you – and so is Alice! We two elderly women keep in close touch, as I'm sure you would expect. And as I think I've told you, I'm expecting Alice to come here soon for a visit. I have been missing you so much, dear Jennifer – I'm sure you know that, though I shouldn't be saying that now – sorry – don't pay attention to this Old Woman! My will-power is weak!!! And there are so many people so much worse off than me. Not just here in Hamilton, or in Ontario, or Canada. There's almost a feeling of increasing panic, I think – listening to the CBC this morning, all those elderly people troubled or hurting or lonely, and sometimes very brave, and some of them angry too – angry with the Seniors' Homes or Hospitals – which are very under-staffed now too. What will come of it all? – So much is troubling. And, oh dear, here I am depressing you, and myself, again – sorry!

What other news was there? Well, fighting, in Afghanistan I think it was – many casualties. Trump still behaving like a spoilt child with a tantrum, but it's getting serious because apparently he's refusing to behave as he should and hand over very important information to the new Administration. What else? To be honest, I can't focus my mind on those –

Jennifer, please, *please*. When you get this email – Just send me a few words because I'm beginning to get very worried! I send you both all my love, dear Jennifer.

Anna: Wednesday 18th November

Dear Alice, thank you so very much for our telephone conversation last night. I was truly troubled, maybe even more than I said, and you calmed me down. I'm sending these few words now, in the morning before I have my breakfast and go out to do a little shop (just a few things in the supermarket, bread, vegs etc), and before I write another email to Jennifer. *Calmly,* as you said – no point in worrying her, troubling her unnecessarily. I wonder if they're having some problem with the car? But that wouldn't explain about no emails. Or maybe – oh, I mustn't – but it's – maybe a crash? If there's snow and ice –

Sorry, Alice. No more – I'll get on with things and I'll call you tonight. I don't really know why I've been getting so worried, maybe it's because I never married and had children? Oh – sorry. Have a good day! I'm sending this early in the morning.

Anna: Wednesday 18th November
Here I am again, dear Jennifer. If only I could hear your voice – or get an email from you! I never thought of saying that you could telephone me and reverse the charges, if they still do that – the Bell Telephone company, I mean. But perhaps you don't remember my telephone number. I don't think you used the phone so very often when you were here. Oh, but now I remember you put the number in your iPhone so you can call me from Vancouver. It would be wonderful to hear your voice, dear Jennifer! So, especially if you're having a problem – Oh, if only I could telephone *you!*

And just at the moment I have so much to tell you; and it's mostly cheerful, unlike the things that were depressing me yesterday – and last night; I actually dreamed, which I rarely do these days!

So – *Jane Goodall!* I know you love that name, and that wonderful woman, as much as I do – I remember we talked about her once, her work with gorillas in Africa and saving animals and working to save the planet! And here she is, working with Senator Murray Sinclair here in Canada to save old circus-elephants, and gorillas I think. And the announcer said there had been a huge number of telephone-calls about saving dogs and other animals here, after a programme about domestic animals being abused. And *then* there was another wonderful name I'm sure you'll remember – *Michael J. Fox*, the film-star who has Parkinson's, and he has just recovered from a fall and an operation on his spine. He was so amazingly cheerful, and used the word 'celebration' as he was talking about his life and his wife and family. He's 59 years old now, with loving wife and children, but he was also, as he said, "candid about mortality" and "days I can't control", and said "at some point you need to exit … and then you die" – which sounds sad but wasn't! The book he has just written (dictated?) and published is called "No Time like the Future", which obviously refers to his most famous movie, but it made me think of you too, and our past and future together! Oh, Jennifer – of course it made me long all the more to be in touch with you! But sorry, I won't nag. And I'll try not to worry.

And that wasn't the end of the lovely and optimistic things this morning. As I was getting up, there was more on the radio. Discussion of a new book about saving the planet from global-warming, saying that Canada may produce only 1.6% of pollution, but per capita in gas-emission it's *second highest in the world* and must make better efforts to fulfil the responsibility we accepted at the U.N. – I expect you're thinking 'Enough, enough!' – Sorry, it's my lack of self-control, with relief from other worries. But there are still great worries about COVID of course: 891 Canadians have died of it so far this month (I think I'm remembering that right) – 'a rising death-toll in Ontario', and even in Nunavut, where they had no cases until now but will be closing down for two weeks! BUT also some good news: there are two promising possible vaccines! Let's hope and pray that at least one is successful and can soon be widely used and stop the spread of COVID. And we'll have to hope that meanwhile, and especially over Christmas and New Year's, people will still take the precautions – especially about social-distancing and wearing masks and not congregating in large groups. It's all so hard on the very young, isn't it? – all this isolation and restraint! (I'm so glad that you two have each other and are away from crowds, travelling – and I'm sure you are careful whenever you stop for a meal or to spend the night in a motel – I was so relieved when Ken told me not to worry, he had more than enough money for your meals and accommodation.)

Anna: Thursday 18th November

Temperature is minus-5 this morning! And there have been high winds, with some snow, in and around Toronto. So Winter really *is* here. And, dear Jennifer, I hope you and Ken are all right, keeping safe and warm enough – wherever you are, I hope in Vancouver, or nearly there if you're still travelling. I'm looking at my telephone and willing it to ring! Then I'll hear your voice and all my worry will be over: you'll tell me I'm a silly old coot, worrying unnecessarily – not in so many words, you would never be so rude, but just hearing your voice – and then I'll know you are all right and I can relax. Of course I will let Alice know immediately and then she can tell me I can "calm down now!" Now I'll have my breakfast.

I'm not feeling so good this afternoon. But I came to a decision and I hope it won't cause any problem – I telephoned the Police, and told them I was worried because I haven't heard from you since you left here nearly two weeks ago. They were polite and took down details, and said they would make immediate enquiries and get back to me as soon as they could. They didn't sound very engaged, I thought – but I guess that's their professional demeanour (is that the right word?). Now I just have to wait. I telephoned Alice as usual last night and she said to be patient a little while longer, but I couldn't!

Anyway, I hope you are both fine. And I'll calm myself by telling you today's news. In the U.S.A., an average of 1,000 deaths from COVID every day, and their Medical Expert says they *must* have a uniform strategy (but how can they have that when Trump won't accept his defeat and get out of the way?); they have 166,000 new COVID cases today! A 'dire' situation, someone said, and it obviously is! Here in Canada, over 300,000 cases so far, over 1,000 new cases in Ontario with 550 in Toronto, and over 11,000 deaths (nearly 1,000 this month). These figures just confuse me, just make the effects of COVID *very* alarming! And they say the feared Second Wave is just beginning. Even in Nunavut, which had no cases the other day, there are now about 60. And there is talk about 'community spread' (which means they can't trace or control it effectively?) and about 'COVID Fatigue' (more and more people just refusing to take precautions?). And so on. Sorry if I'm depressing you, alarming you. This is the world we are living in, though, isn't it?

But, my dear Jennifer, PLEASE send me a reply. PLEASE.

Anna: Thursday 19th November
Hullo, Alice. I think I've been making mistakes over the date: sorry, Alice, if so! Maybe I should stop sending you emails – I mean, separately from sending you copies of the

ones I've been sending to Jennifer. Please let me know. But now that I've contacted the Police – I did understand what you advised, *so sorry about that*, too, Alice – I just *could not go on*, worrying and worrying – I'm not as tough as you are! And when we talk on the phone I just lose it; somehow just hearing your voice sets me off – why am I so weak now, when I've had self-control through most of my life? I remember when Boris would say cutting things to me, I would be upset of course, but keep it inside and just smile. Maybe now I'm really – But I know it's also about Jennifer, about her leaving, and so suddenly – and with Ken – I confess that I never really liked him, he always seemed to despise me, and sometimes I even thought that he was trying to turn James against me – but then, after James died – and I couldn't even be there, with him, in the hospital, and we had been good friends for so long – he was always kind and pleasant with me –

Oh, sorry, Alice. You'll be thinking I'm so weak and feeble. Sorry. But *please* don't be upset with me about contacting the Police. I had such a horrible nightmare last night, it just went on and on, and I thought I was running and screaming, and maybe I *was* screaming, and eventually I switched on the light and got up and put on my dressing-gown. Oh, and you'll be amused at this, I put on the CD of the Schubert Quintet, the slow movement that I love, and I just listened to it over and over, three times I think, until I felt calm; and then I went back to bed, and got some sleep at last. It was strange – weird, as my students would say, some of them. And maybe you would say too!

Anyway, I won't bother you more now. I prefer emailing you, if you don't mind. But it's lovely to hear your voice too!

Anna: Friday 20th November

Last night I tried to distract myself a bit from worrying – so I turned on the TV and watched for a while. The News was of course very troubling, as it always is now – though at least there is the hope for a COVID vaccine becoming available before too many more Seniors have died, in Long-term care or Hospitals – where there is growing concern, especially as Staff fall ill. This morning on the CBC there was the very sad story of a middle-aged teacher, diligent and loving, who has just died. But back to last night: I made a bad mistake, deciding to watch a drama that I thought would distract me, *The Poison Tree* – well, I should have switched it off before it poisoned *me*; it was full of anger and fear and violence, all the emotions that are becoming so prevalent now, and which can only do further damage to us.

But I shouldn't write this sort of stuff, Jennifer. Sorry. Wish I had cheerful topics. Oh, there *is* one. I had to go out this morning to shop, I was beginning to run out of everything! If you go early enough, you don't even have to line up, and I met a friend and had a conversation with her (suitably distant, of course); and you know, that almost made my day! She asked after you – I can't recall her name (my decaying memory!) but I'm sure you'll remember her, plump and she has an Italian accent. These days, when one can't even go into one anothers' houses, meetings like that really matter. – But you can see I haven't got much to say that's worth saying, dear Jennifer. There'd be so much more to talk about if – Well, no point in being miserable, wanting more than we can have.

So I'll say goodbye, my love to you both!

Anna: Friday 20th November

Oh Alice. This will be short. I promised to tell you. So I must.

Early this afternoon, there was a knock at my door. People usually ring the bell, so I wondered and my heart just dropped and I nearly fainted. When I opened the door, it was a Police Officer, wearing a mask of course, which frightened me for a moment but then I could tell, I don't know how, that it wasn't good news, he was – Oh Alice – Because he looked –

And he said I should sit down and so I did. Then he told me. Oh Alice. Ken is *dead*. I don't think I heard everything else he said, I started crying, and he went into the kitchen and brought me some water. Then he said should he arrange for me to have company, and support, as I'm alone? but all I could think of was Jennifer and was she all right? they must tell me, I begged him to, and then he said they don't even know where she is, they're looking for her, and I think then I just collapsed and he must have called for someone to come, and it was a young woman officer, she was very pleasant, and calm, and then when he went, and he said he'd come back later, she helped me to get into bed and I just lay there and tried not to cry. And I must have dropped off eventually.

In the evening, they brought me some food and I tried to eat some, but I wanted them to tell me everything, and they said that all they know so far is that Ken's car was just off the highway, in the bush, someone had reported that to the local Police, and when they investigated they found Ken – he had been shot, he was dead, and his body had been dragged into the bush.

I'm telling you all this, dear Alice, because I promised to. But I can't even do it properly. My mind is so full of worrying and worrying about Jennifer, I can't think straight. If only I could – But I gave your address to the Police, I hope you don't mind, they wanted to know the names of my nearest relatives, and of course I don't have any, and the names of my nearest friends.

Anna, dear Anna, I am so sorry. I can't say how sorry. I wish I could be with you. It's like a nightmare, I can hardly believe it, Ken murdered and where is Jennifer. What a truly horrible thing to happen, and in the midst of this nightmare of COVID-19 too, when there is so much suffering and death wherever one looks. I wish I could say something helpful and consoling, I just wish we could be together and I could hug you and so we could talk quietly together. Dear Anna!

And now I feel bad too. I should have told you before. I've been saying that I'll visit you in Hamilton, and I truly did want to, and intended to – especially when the three Chinese students decided to leave. But something's happened, that I never expected. I'll tell you just briefly – About a week ago, there was a knock at the back door, and it was a young refugee woman (from Syria, I found that out later, she had only a few words of English). I could see immediately that she was pregnant, and she needed food and somewhere to stay, so I did what you would have done – I invited her in and gave her food and said in sign-language she could stay for a while and I took her up to the bedroom on the second floor (the one you and Jennifer were in, when we were all together for the Schubert Quintet). Only until things are worked out with the Authorities. And she gave me a telephone number on a piece of paper, so I could leave a message for her husband to tell him where she was. She didn't have much English, as I said. And then I also noticed that she was pregnant. She was very shy, and exhausted I think.

But, Anna, don't think there isn't room for you! Of

course there is. There are the other two bedrooms, or you could even sleep where Boris used to sleep, before he was in the wheelchair (you could even sleep in *that*, it's still here!!! In the basement, I think). So *come*, dear Anna, whenever you can! I long to see you and have another of our lovely long conversations!

But of course I know that now is not the time for anything but mourning Ken, and finding Jennifer. Forgive me if I seem to have been light-hearted, I don't feel like that at all – and *please keep me in the picture* – or ask the Police to let me know. What a dreadful shock for you! Please look after yourself. How I wish I could be with you, dear Anna! You are strong, I know, but it's so hard and painful for you. I'm thinking and praying for you.

My love – Alice

Anna: Saturday 21st November

Dear Alice, thank you for your email. I found it after I got up a little while ago, it's now early afternoon, nearly three o'clock, I don't think I ever stayed in bed for a whole morning, or not since I was a girl with measles or mumps or whatever, but I had a very bad night, restless, and I hardly slept at all, and if I did it was full of nightmares about Jennifer and Ken – oh, poor Ken, I can't bear to think of him, in pain, and dying like that – and Jennifer, where is she, and I hardly dare to – is she alive, *where is she*? Sorry, Alice – I'm upsetting you. And myself. And, dear Alice, I won't telephone you, I know I would break down and not be able to talk, so I'll do what I'm doing, just send you emails. From now on.

When I woke up this morning and switched on my bedside radio, as I do every morning, I almost switched it straight off – The CBC News was mostly about how COVID is spreading again in most Provinces – here in Ontario we are going into Lockdown (Toronto, and now here, Hamilton), to try to control this Second Wave – warnings from the PM, Trudeau, and that Dr Theresa Tam and also our Premier, Ford, to stay indoors, no gatherings and wear masks, and so on – and restaurant closures etcetera and how the doctors and nurses in hospitals are *exhausted*, and most patients sicker on arrival in hospitals than before, and so how – There was a call-in programme too, and one poor woman who was a hair-dresser, with her own small-business, she was almost in tears, one could tell, at being shut-down again – And I just lay there, and wept too with her. And all the others. So many businesses shut down and may never open again. And so many people worrying about their financial situation – I'm one of the lucky ones, with a pension and no dependants. Will we ever go back to normal? And Jennifer and Ken. Oh, please, please – Jennifer. And I thought about how Boris thought the world was ending – how he even believed it *should* end, because human-beings have been so destructive and stupid and irresponsible.

But now I'm up and dressed and had a bit to eat and a cup of tea. And now what do I do?

Alice, did I say I'll *email* you, like this, now, not tele-phone? – I'll just weep if I try to talk, I know.

I haven't answered your email, I know. Sorry. I hope that poor pregnant refugee woman – I know you'll look after her, does she have a husband?

I must stop. Dear Alice, I send my love.

That Police-woman telephoned again, and of course she gave me her number yesterday – and said if I have any need at all, I must call, she would come immediately – they're being very kind, but oh I hoped when I heard her voice that they might have news about Jennifer – though I also feel frightened, if it's bad news –

Thanks for your email, Anna. I'm writing this on Saturday night. What you suggested, about emailing rather than telephoning, is fine – in fact, it's better, isn't it? We can do it at any time, and you don't even have to hear it and run for it or even know about it until you look at your email!

I just wanted to hope you are all right. Have you heard anything more? I'm longing to hear that Jenny is all right. I'm thinking that the fact she wasn't there with Ken, or in the car, is a good sign that she's all right. Someone may have picked her up, she could have run along the highway. If she was in any *danger*, I mean.

Also I wanted to say again: Do come and stay, dear Anna! Surely the Police will be able to bring you here, if you ask them. And don't please think that there isn't room for you, I tried to say that. The two refugees seem to have settled in, and are very pleasant and friendly. She's Maria and he's Mario – I call them 'MandM'! But not to their faces! Their baby is due next month. I telephoned our Doctor, the one Boris liked so much, who medically-assisted his death. I don't think you met her, but she is very nice and immediately said Yes, of course, she would love to deliver the baby – of course Mario could be at work when it happens; his uncle employs him, and he often has to work at night. Anyway, I just wanted to keep you in the picture. I'll have to go to the supermarket for a big shop this afternoon – people will be starting to panic if there's going to be a Lockdown from next week.

Anna, I worry about you. And I feel so helpless. I guess you do, too – even more than me. Are the Police really trying hard to locate Jenny, do you think? Please tell me if I can do anything to help. And please know how welcome you would be here. After all, we both knew Boris for so long! And we are cousins, however distant! And old friends. But Jenny – I remember she said both her parents were dead, didn't she say that? And of course the uncle in Vancouver will have been contacted by the Police? I wonder if somehow she reached the uncle, maybe, or sent him a message?

Anna: Saturday 21st November

Oh, Alice, I didn't even think about trying to contact Jennifer's uncle. And I should have: he is probably worrying about her too, why she hasn't arrived? But I don't have his phone number – I don't even know his name, just Wiseman, I think she mentioned that's his surname – I'll tell the Police and maybe – Jennifer said she'd give me her uncle's full name and address, but somehow everything was a rush when Ken arrived, and he wanted to leave immediately but I persuaded them to at least stay the night and have a good breakfast before they left; he slept on the chesterfield. Oh, why didn't I ask for details about her uncle – but I expected we would be regularly emailing each other after they left.

Anyway, there has been one development. The Police telephoned to say that *her iPhone has been found*! though not anywhere close to Ken and the car or where they searched – actually someone handed it in to a police-station a few kilometres further on towards Vancouver, apparently. Said he'd found it at the side of the road near his house. And they say it has my messages to Jennifer in it, along with a few others, but of course no messages by her to me. But why *didn't* she email me? Angela (that's the kind Policewoman who has been in regular contact with me) – she says maybe the iPhone had slipped down under her seat and she thought she'd lost it – that happened to *her* once, Angela said – and when Jennifer found it she took a chance to throw it out of the car. As a sign. If she was desperate – Angela didn't say that but I thought it. But of course I can't know what actually happened, and they still have no idea where Jennifer is. But they said at least it indicates that somehow she got a way further than where they found Ken and the car. Oh, Alice. What does it all mean? Just makes me more worried –

Thank you for inviting me (again!). That's so kind. Today I'm feeling a bit better. My Mother always said to eat a good breakfast, so I did. It's a dismal day, grey and rainy, but I went for a walk and the exercise has helped. But the worrying just goes on. And the COVID news is always there too: I think they said that, in this Second Wave just starting, Ontario's daily number is already over 2,000? Getting so high, and it seems that some people are still not taking it seriously and behaving responsibly. So now we're going into Lockdown from tonight, Toronto and even here, Hamilton, for I think two weeks! I hope you won't have too big a burden, Alice – looking after that young pregnant refugee; I wish I was there to give you some help! And that might take my mind off worrying and worrying about Jennifer.

Anyway – my love, Alice. You know – I was going to say we're 'the last two' (now that Boris, James and Ken are gone) but no, that was stupid and thoughtless, of course there's Jennifer too, we are the last *three*. But where is she? Oh, Jennifer, Jennifer.

Anna: Sunday 22nd November
Oh, what a miserable day, grey and rainy! And snow – the first snow of winter! But of course it hasn't lasted long, and

now there's not even a dusting. I'll go for a walk soon – just along the sidewalk: must get some exercise, I'm getting so stiff.

I heard on the CBC News a little while ago that Ontario has 1,500 new cases of COVID. And there are 325,000 cases altogether, 5,000 of them new cases, across Canada, with four provinces setting new records (which almost makes it sound positive) – And in the U.S.A., 12 million new cases! – can that be right? – and Trump and his lot are still trying to overturn his loss to Biden – *disgraceful!*). No wonder people are getting panicky, everywhere – but we *must* all try to keep control of ourselves. There is increasing concern, here, of course, about overcrowded hospitals, and about the medical community – doctors and nurses who are totally exhausted. Boris, is this the Coming End? – No, you would be enjoying the lovely music that I've been listening to with one ear, on the CBC, including some favourites of mine – Smetana's *Vltava*, Ravel's cheerful jagged Piano Concerto in G.

Lunch! Tea! My Mother always said Put some food in your stomach, drink a hot cup of tea, and the world will improve immediately! Then I'll get out there for a walk.

Anna: Sunday 22nd November

I'm back. Yes, it was chilly out there! And hardly anybody around, all cowering indoors!

But I have news, and thank goodness it's positive. Not from or about Jennifer, alas, but positive. Earlier there was a call from Angela to check that I'm all right, and to say – Well, it was essentially the same as an email message that I found when I got in from my walk. *Jennifer's uncle*!!! His name is Noel Wiseman, so at least I remembered his surname correctly! He said we must talk; he has my telephone number from the iPhone, the Police gave it to him, and he will call tonight. But it was clear from what Angela said that he had nothing significant to say, just that Jennifer had recently written to him, and he had invited her and her friend (obviously Ken but she hadn't told him her friend's name) to stay with him and his wife and son in Vancouver. It was many years (about ten, he said) since he had seen her, when she visited them soon after immigrating to Canada; but she hadn't stayed very long and hadn't been in touch with them since. But he remembered her telling him that, after the War, and then the deaths of her parents (her mother was his sister, apparently) she had lived with an aunt, who taught her to play the cello. He and his family had been looking forward to Jennifer's visit. I called Angela back, as she had asked, and we agreed that she would come round this evening. She is such a pleasant person, especially as a Policewoman (joke!). So I'll have my supper and be ready for her. I'll let you know what she says, if she has anything new to say (she must know about Noel Wiseman of course, and maybe, I hope so, she'll have more to tell me).

Well, Angela came and went, and Noel Wiseman telephoned as he said he would. But it wasn't a very happy conversation as we are both so worried about Jennifer. He wants to see Jennifer's iPhone, and the Police said they would first have to check it thoroughly for any clues to her whereabouts etcetera. They'll let *me* know as well as him, I hope, about any information they find. I said that to Angela. Oh, if only there's *something*, some clue at least. Angela didn't have any more information, and I really think she would tell me anything significant if she possibly could. Noel Wiseman said he is a businessman and travels a lot, and he's married and has a son. I think I've told you everything now.

Anna: Monday 23rd November

It's sunny this morning, but chilly of course! I decided to drive up the Dundas Valley for a walk, and it was truly lovely, the trees covered with snow (which had been covered with red and yellow leaves not so long ago): a different type of beauty now, but so calming for me. I have a lot to think about, lots of things to tell you, dear Alice, and so now I'll try to write them. (For myself, too – it helps!)

But I must remember to send you my love first: I'm so grateful to have you as a friend – I'd be so lonely otherwise, and I have always had to fight Depression (my Mother always said I would have to do that, "You're like your Father, always seeing the bad side of things" she used to say).

Anyway, first about Mr Noel Wiseman. My impression now is that he is a very forceful man, and he is determined to find Jennifer, he really *is* committed, and won't take No for an answer! That was a relief. I think he's probably rich and influential. He wants to meet us, and of course I tried to say he would be very welcome, but present circumstances, with COVID etcetera, will presumably be a barrier.

And, thinking and talking of COVID (as we are forced to do now, at nearly every moment of our lives it seems!), I heard that it's getting very bad again, in this so-called Second Wave that seems to be breaking over us – even in the Maritimes now, in what they called 'The Atlantic Bubble'; according to the CBC News this morning, they're having to take special measures to prevent COVID spread. Oh and I got it wrong, Alice, and should apologise – here in Hamilton we're *not* Locked Down, or not *yet*, as you are in Toronto – on the CBC News there was a lot about how your total lockdown is causing distress, especially to Businesses, and yesterday great crowds were doing panic-shopping downtown. I wondered if you – of course, with two extra mouths to feed now, you must need extra provisions. Oh, I wish I could help, Alice! Please look after yourself – and I hope your two refugees, I can't remember their names, Maria was the woman, I think you said – anyway, I hope they are all right too. But I was saying, *we* are not doing well now, either, with COVID, in Hamilton, and I'm thinking I must be more careful, and wear the mask *all the time* when I'm outside etcetera –

But this morning, I woke up later than usual again, and just lay in bed for a while, listening to the radio and thinking, trying to be calm. And it did help a lot to hear Barack Obama's voice – he was being interviewed, in connection with his just-published autobiography, and he *laughed* a few times, he *laughed*! There was no malice at all, in anything he said, and he actually commented on making mistakes when he was President, on actually being *wrong!* And I thought what a joy not to be hearing lies and vindictiveness and slimy cheap gibes, one could go on and on about the sheer *nastiness* of Trump that we've had to endure for four years – and the whole of the U.S.A. has been so demeaned nationally and internationally, surely Americans *must* know that! But I won't say any more about it. Just upsets me!

Also on the same programme, with Matt Galloway, who is such a very decent and *excellent* broadcaster (we're so lucky to have him, I know you would agree), there was an item that would interest you as much as me: the 'murder rampage' in Nova Scotia, when we were performing the Schubert Quintet: it happened just before we learned, I think, that dear Boris had committed suicide – well, I'm putting it badly, sorry – and of course *you* knew about his decision before that – to ask his doctor to give him a medically-assisted suicide. Anyway – Did you know those murders were 'the worst mass-killing in

Canadian history'! One of the men, whose pregnant wife was murdered, he was hardly able to talk about it in the interview, he was so consumed with anger about what he said was the failure of the R.C.M.P. to alert the community. I think I told you, at the time it happened, that it was not very far from where I was born and grew up, in Nova Scotia, near Truro. Like now, there was so much intensity, in my mind and all around me, at that time, I felt very upset and confused. That poem that Boris loved, *Abt Vogler* by Robert Browning (how often he would quote from it! and especially he would declaim "the C Major of this life"!) – I always remember especially one line, "Why rushed the discords in, but that harmony should be prized?" I think that's how it goes. But is there *ever* harmony in our lives, I wonder – except in short bursts, very occasionally! And we're living in very *dissonant* times, aren't we?

Anyway, I mustn't ramble on and on, dear Alice. Maybe you've already stopped reading my drivel (that's what my Father sometimes said to me, "Stop that driveling, Anna – *at once!*"). But it does give me harmony, Alice, talking to you like this. I look forward to hearing from you, my dear friend! And I feel almost like a traitor when I think and talk about anything or anyone other than Jennifer – yet I think I would go mad if that was the only thing and it drowned out everything else. And I think she would agree with that! But dear Jennifer, where are you, where are you? Where *are* you?

Alice: Monday 23rd November

Getting towards the end of the month, and only a few weeks to Christmas now! And what sort of Christmas will it be this year, when we can't gather together as family and friends for meals and conversation and sociability, or go to

Church. But obviously we will just have to make the best of it.

You asked about my Guests, Anna. We are all doing well. Dr Galbraith says Maria's pregnancy is going well, but her husband seems to worry about her a lot, he's protective and seems to love her deeply – but he's clearly pleased to have good work, in this desperate time when so many are losing or have lost their work. He said, in his remarkably good English, that they're grateful to be here in this house, and he has even been able to contribute to our household expenses, which is good for his pride. (Don't think from that that I am struggling financially – I'm not, Boris had good savings and he made sure that I am well-provided-for – in fact, I feel guilty when I hear about so many people struggling now, worrying about the future – whatever it will be.)

I'm so glad to know that Jenny's uncle has contacted you and seems to be just as committed to finding her. Anna, I don't want to cause you any further worry, so ignore this if it does – What I want to ask is, do the Police have any idea who the abductor is? Surely his vehicle, you said it was left there, next to poor Ken, didn't you – and they would be able to trace ownership, and find out about him? Maybe they don't want to worry you, and I hope *I'm* not worrying you – but is he a *local*? – I guess I'm thinking that – well, you said there's more coming out now about the dreadful murders in Nova Scotia that we both remember all too well. I'm sure the RCMP have found out everything they could – so one hopes that they are on the trail and will soon find him – and Jenny.

I'm so sorry we can't be together, Anna. As I said, of course you are always welcome here – and the more I get to know them, the better I like Maria and her husband. She's so gentle, and always helpful and grateful, and he's charming and very responsible – a hard worker and much older than her but I can see he loves her deeply! But I'm repeating my-self, I think!

So let's keep in touch this way, as you said. I miss hearing your voice, though, so I hope you'll phone me sometimes, and if you don't *I'll* have to phone *you*! Dear Anna!

By the way, we had a very big snowfall yesterday – the snow-ploughs had a hard time, and so did many pedestrians and vehicles today! I was glad I could stay indoors! Did you have much snow in Hamilton?

TWO

Anna: Wednesday 25th November

Alice, here I am! It was good to talk to you last night when you telephoned. I'm sorry that I just took the day off, so to speak: decided that I was close to collapsing. Yes, I am *feeble*, aren't I? Too much worrying, not only about Jennifer, but also about the COVID situation, now becoming so dire eve-rywhere in Canada (I heard on the CBC that all three ex-tremes of the country, the West (BC), the East (Maritimes) and Nunavut, are now affected, with rapidly-rising numbers of infection and death, and their Provincial Governments having to take drastic measures; and I've just heard that Al-berta, which in the recent past has been the least, or one of the least, afflicted Provinces, has declared a Public Health Emer-gency!). And across the border, in the U.S., huge crowds are travelling, in crowded planes and airports, for their Thanks-giving Day, tomorrow I think it is. One fears a huge toll of infection and deaths. Oh, Boris –

Anyway, I'm feeling better now, after a good long sleep (I was exhausted and just collapsed after your call – and Jennifer's Uncle's, he called a bit later than you, when I was having supper. It's yet another dreary day, as you will well know; and actually I'm wondering if you're still having problems, trees down and power-cuts etcetera, after your storm – which we in Hamilton escaped almost entirely! Earlier yesterday I had to shop for provisions, and also went for quite a long walk along beside the Lake. And I played my violin a lot – many of the Bach pieces I love, especially the six sonatas and partitas, so beautiful and energetic and calming: I always think I'm so lucky to have music! I said that once or twice to Boris in the old days, when I was young and defenceless and excitable, and he would just turn those eyebrows at me and grunt.

So let me catch you (and me) up about yesterday.

I forgot to say that there was a *third* telephone-call – before yours. From Angela, the Policewoman who is so kind and thoughtful: she seems to have decided that I need calming and encouraging (which I do!), or maybe she just has been told to check up on me regularly: anyway, we seem to have almost become friends, and I know now that she's married (to a fellow-officer) and has a small daughter who is looked-after during the day by her sister (her mother died last year). She has talked to colleagues in Vancouver about Jennifer's uncle; and it seems that he really *is* wealthy and quite prominent and well-known, one of those "Oil Barons", is that what they're called? – though I guess now is not such a good time for them either.

Then *he* called, and finally *you* did. I was so glad to hear that all is well with you and your two guests: maybe I'll meet them one day soon, if I can get to Toronto and visit you – but that seems less and less likely to be possible, at least until next year sometime. In fact it seems almost certain, doesn't it, that there'll be no travelling or socializing over Christmas and New Year's.

On the CBC News today, further increases of COVID here in Hamilton, so no doubt we will soon be in Lockdown like you. Oh, no, of course I didn't feel upset by your queries about Jennifer: I just wish, so much, for both of us, that there was some *news*. That they find her, *soon*. But I really think the Uncle, Noel – he said to call him by his Christian name, when we talked last night, and he sounded – well, quite authoritative (or do I mean authoritarian?), and he said how his son has already set out to where Ken's body had been found. Apparently, the son has very good memories of Jennifer: she looked after him when he was a boy, when she visited them soon after she came to Canada – his Mother had just gone off with another man, apparently. And Noel also said, last night, that he would be coming to Hamilton very soon, and maybe his wife will come too, she was his Secretary before they married and remembers Jennifer. He has a private airplane, so he could land here at our airport, he says. He promised that he'll let me know his arrangements very soon. I asked if he would tell his son to please telephone or email me as soon as he finds anything more out – and he said he would of course, and that he was in close touch with the RCMP.

So that's where it's at, as they say. I wish so much that there was some real *news* – or, best of all, that we could be in touch with Jennifer, talk to her – it's so hard to be cut-off like this, wondering and worrying! But then I think, well, it's just like what so many people have had to endure, and are still enduring, separated from elderly relatives in Seniors' Homes – and of course the poor Seniors there are virtually imprisoned, in near-isolation – and then I remember also that, sadly, there have been so many deaths among those isolated elderly grandparents and other relatives, and that's still happening, and I try to think of other things – It's such a consolation to write or talk to you, dear Alice. I am so grateful and so fortunate.

After saying all that, I shouldn't comment on recent COVID news – except that they're saying now it seems very possible that there will be not one but *three* Vaccines soon; though they're also saying it will take time to distribute them etcetera, so one shouldn't be over-optimistic; on the other side, though, there is the rapidly-rising infection-rate and death-toll across Canada, and of course in the U.S.A. and elsewhere, and the near-certainty that Christmas, the loveliest, most hopeful celebration of all, will be almost cancelled (well, as a communal occasion. When I was growing up, we would attend the Christmas Midnight Mass, as a family; and I still remember, with such delight, one Christmas Day that began with a gentle snowfall just as we were emerging from the Church – what a joyful memory, and how fortunate I am to have it!).

So now I'll bid farewell, dear Alice. My love to you and your little immigrant family.

Alice: Wednesday 25th November

Yes, Anna. Thanks for your email. All good here – in spite of the current depressive Way of the World. Maria is right now washing-up after our supper. Which makes her more than worth her weight in gold! By the way, she asked me to send you their greetings (her husband is away at work – has to take a bus-ride, wouldn't hear of me paying for it). She seemed very struck when I told her about your joyful memory of Christmas Midnight Mass, and she said, I could see she was trying to say, that she has similar memories. Of course I would like to take her to the local Catholic church for a

Christmas service, but there are obviously two major strikes against that – her pregnancy, which as I probably told you is very advanced, and the fact that all churches have been physically closed to their congregations for a while. She remains cheerful and carefully active. A lovely young woman, I just wish we could communicate better. If only I spoke her language, or her English was better!

What else? You know how I'm like you, also longing to hear from Jenny. It's so hard to be patient, isn't it – and especially, I shouldn't say this but I'm sure it's been in your mind, too – especially now that Winter is here. I've never been good at praying, but I *have* been praying and praying, as I'm sure you have been also, praying that she has good shelter. That young man, her cousin (do you know his name?), who is looking for her, I hope he finds her quickly. The RCMP must be looking too, maybe he has joined them. Maybe she was confused and just wandered away – oh no, that's not – What does your friend the Woman-policeman say? What about the man who shot poor Ken and must have abducted Jenny? I know we both don't want to think about that, but I can't help it – forgive me, Anna if –

So I'm hoping and praying, Anna. I know you'll keep me informed. Please remember I'm right beside you as much as I can be. And now *Sleep Well* – you need your sleep!

Anna: Thursday 26th November

Yes, I did sleep quite well – you are so insistent and I am so obedient! Neither of us can avoid thinking about Jennifer and wondering what is happening, so of course I'm not upset by anything you say, dear Alice. I'm thinking that maybe *today* there'll be news that they have found her. Please, God! If I hear anything, you know I'll let you know immediately – I'll telephone as well to be sure.

But meanwhile, during this waiting, waiting, waiting – On today's News on the CBC, and in discussion afterwards, there was a lot about the Vaccines that are being developed A.S.A.P.; but one of the three "front-runners" has run into problems, and who knows about the other two? It also sounds increasingly like a huge international competition to make money and control distribution, with of course the poorest countries getting any vaccine last or even not at all. And now heated political arguments in Canada about Why are we "at the back of the line"? – "it's contrary to what the Government's been saying" – and who is responsible? etcetera: all nasty politics! And cases of COVID soaring, right across Canada: over 1,350 new cases and 35 more deaths in Ontario yesterday, 500+ deaths so far in Alberta, or is that in *Canada*, and globally 60 million cases of COVID and going on for 2 million deaths! – I hope I've got that right; it's all bewildering (at least for me, with my confused brain that can hardly add 2 and 2 – I am going to stop even *trying* to keep up with what is clearly a *huge spread* of COVID in the U.S. and in many countries around the world – and now beginning here in Canada, and, as I think I said, there are political struggles beginning, in this Province and Alberta, according to today's news, with their Governments accused of "political interference" in policy and practice, etcetera – failing to "manage their response" to COVID and prevent the increasing number of deaths, especially of Seniors).

Did I say it's another damp grey day? Well, it is. But you'll know that, I assume!

Oh, Alice, what a sad and depressing time we are living through.

There! I'm making myself miserable again! If you're still reading this, please forgive me. I'm going to have my lunch, then go out to shop, my cupboard is almost bare! And that will also be my exercise of the day, walking there and back (of course I still have the car, but I only take it out now for a big weekly shop, to keep it happy!). The Park is now a bit wet and muddy, so I don't walk there so much.

Anna: Thursday 26th November

Alice – it's Anna again. I said I'd telephone you, didn't I, and I will, a bit later. But there is some NEWS: not what we are most anxious to hear, but positive, I think.

First, I had a call from Noel's son. His name is Christopher, by the way. He was telephoning from near the Manitoba-Saskatchewan border, I think – where Jennifer's iPhone was found. Ken's car has been found near a farm-road, not far from the Highway. And some distance from where Ken and the other vehicle were. The Police have let Christopher see the iPhone, and he was also able to join their search. Unfortunately, he said, snow has covered whatever tracks there had been. But at least they have found the car! Which, as I said, had been driven off the Highway onto a farm-road, and abandoned there – driven or pushed off the farm-road.

Apparently the Police are puzzled, just like me, over why Jennifer never sent any emails – all mine to *her* are there on her iPhone, of course, Christopher said. But she must have thought she'd lost the iPhone, when it had just slipped under the car-seat maybe? That happened to me once. And that man who killed poor Ken and abducted Jennifer, he forced her back into the car if she'd got out – and then he apparently drove Ken's car much further along the highway, Jennifer must have been terrified – until he turned off onto the farm-road where the car was discovered, pushed just off the road, and then he must have forced her to walk with him, but they don't know where to – they're going to all the farms nearby, asking for information. It's a big farming community, Christopher said, with many temporary farm-workers who haven't been able to go home to their various countries because of COVID.

The farmer who saw Ken's car as he was driving up the road towards the highway reported it to the nearest police-station. He said he hadn't noticed the car earlier when he drove past it – "that farm-road's very rough," he said, "you can't take your eyes off of it", and it was snowing too. He said he hadn't seen Jennifer or the man who had abducted her; and the Police haven't made contact either – Christopher says they're still searching, visiting all the nearby farms, interviewing farmers and workers.

And that's all Christopher could tell me, Alice, but he said he's going to stay there, with a neighbor of the farmer who found Ken's car, he said, until they locate Jennifer. So that sounds – well, it's still horribly worrying but at least there's *some* progress. Surely someone knows something! (Did you ever hear that CBC series? But I shouldn't be light-hearted at all, it's all horribly serious, and until they find Jennifer, how can one rest or really relax at all?) I think I told you the other vehicle had been stolen too? So the Police had nothing to go on before. Am I making sense?

Anna: Friday 27th November

What a miserable day! Chilly, grey. I would have been troubled, anyway, about Jennifer – and about the worsening COVID situation here. I went for a longish walk in the Park this morning (at about 10:30), and then walked on into the centre of Westdale (our suburb of Hamilton, as I think you know?) and there outside the Second Cup sat a few acquaintances drinking coffee and chatting – so I joined them for an hour or so, some of us masked and all at least enacting cheerfulness, while we chattered about anything except the increasing spread of COVID across Canada. The news of vaccines being discovered and becoming available has raised some optimism, but this has now been a bit undermined by awareness of how long it will take for them to be made and disseminated. And also undermined by the political machinations and competition and profit-making.

Now I've had a light lunch (bought outside one of the local restaurants, which are clearly suffering economically) and am back home sitting here at my laptop trying to be cheerful, and hopeful. (And I hope you're in "a better space", as they say, dear Alice – at least better than me: please email me back this evening, or telephone and we'll have a restorative chat?) (But not if you're very busy.)

Another cause of my near-depression: When I got home at lunchtime, I found a copy of a local weekly newspaper (the *Dundas Star News,* delivered free) and brought it inside with me, to put in our Blue Box for disposal on Monday next. Usually I don't read it; but this time a headline caught my attention – "Health System in 'Dire' Situation". The President of Hamilton Health Sciences is quoted as saying that, because of the COVID crisis, our health-care system is "operating more hospital beds than we were funded to operate", has necessarily "performed 4,000 fewer surgeries this year" than in 2019, and hospital-staffing has become "an area of great concern", and operations are being put off – in fact, the whole health-care system is facing "a dire reality", while still suffering from "the impact of the first wave of COVID". And we know that many of the seniors' homes are still struggling – Oh, Alice, I don't want to depress you – I'm sorry. And it's also been reported, just today, that there were over 70 new infections of COVID here yesterday. But I'll say no more about that. What can we do about it anyway?

I must think and pray for our beloved Jennifer, wherever she is. Yes, pray. I don't think we have ever spoken about religion, you and I, but I am remembering how important my Christian belief was to me, when I was a child and young woman (I lost my faith, I always used to say, in my first year of training to be a teacher. Which was in Nova Scotia – not very far from those dreadful murders that were committed when we were performing Schubert's Quintet with Boris, and James, and Ken, and Jennifer, in your house – just a few months ago, but it seems so much longer – and all three of the men are dead now – and Jennifer, Jennifer – where is she? I think I heard on the CBC the other day that it was the worst mass-murder in Canadian history, that one in Nova Scotia earlier this year. And there is a whole hour-long CBC TV programme on it now: should I watch it? Possibly, to know more about what happened; but I know it would be gruelling, and probably troubling too.

I'll stop for a bit now, Alice. Sorry if I've upset you with this dismal email – going on and on in this dreary way. I'll try to be more cheerful later, I promise. And hopefully I'll have better things to communicate!

Anna: Friday 27th November

And now it's 9:30 at night. I'll go to bed soon, and hope to sleep. I decided, after an early supper, to watch some TV, which I haven't done for quite a long time (mainly to protect my eyes as I think my sight is deteriorating). One of my acquaintances, probably trying to cheer me up, mentioned this morning that I would enjoy a programme about gardens: relaxing and informative she said: by Monty Don (I think that's right, doesn't sound like an English name to me, but he was very English, and charming) – one of his series on American Gardens, and it was excellent! And very calming, as she said it would be. But before that I watched (because I wasn't sure of the time for the Gardens programme) the American News, and then Canadian News, which weren't at all calming! In fact, extremely troubling. Would you believe that the U.S.A. now has over 100,000 new COVID cases each day, and 1,500 deaths from COVID each day, and that more than 1,700 U.S. Healthcare workers have died so far of COVID. And the situation in Canada is also getting much worse, of course: about 6,000 new COVID cases, and over 560 COVID deaths, today, across Canada; and 30% of workers in Seniors' Homes have not returned to their work. I noted down those facts, I hope correctly. And apparently more and more people are frightened to go into a hospital to be tested for COVID – and it's now thought that even children can be carriers, while showing no sign of infection – etcetera. But more than enough on that topic: sorry if I've depressed you again, Alice. I'm taking a vow not to include any more COVID commentary in my emails to you! And to try to think of pleasanter things, like Religion; and *do* pleasanter things, like play my violin!

But I intended to tell you about the telephone call last night from Noel Wiseman's wife. I was so surprised to hear her voice: of course I didn't recognize it, didn't know it. She sounded pleasant, her name is Helen, and she said that Noel had asked her to call me and say that Christopher is still searching for Jennifer, with the Police. She explained that she remembered Jennifer well; that she had been Noel's secretary at the time and "Jennifer is such a lovely girl in every way, so beautiful, so talented"; they had all loved her and even hoped that Christopher – "but of course he's younger than her and he was only interested in sport and parties at that time"; but they had all got on so well, and it was only because "things were so confused and tense at that time" in the Wiseman home that Helen thought Jennifer may have felt uncomfortable. She also said that Noel wanted to visit me soon: he has to discuss important business problems with Staff in the company's Toronto office, and he could fly to and from Hamilton and see me, and drive from here to Toronto and back again – he has a private plane, of course! And Helen said she could come with him, she'd like to meet me, if – and of course I said they'd be very welcome at any time: I can easily put them up, and, at the very least, Alice, it would be some relief from all the worrying. So that's where we are now – maybe a bit further forward, though I wonder when there'll be any more news – Christopher hasn't called, and Helen said she thought he had nothing new to report.

Anyway, I'll take myself off to bed now, and hope to sleep. My love to you and your Family, dear Alice. As I said, I think – I am praying so much for Jennifer – and hoping that God will forgive me for my long apostasy (is that the right word? I think so. And spelt right?). So Good Night, dear Friend.

Anna: Saturday 28th November

Well, Alice. Here I am again. I did sleep quite well, but I'm feeling very tense. I'm going to play more Bach this morning – what would I do without my violin and my music?

Anna: Sunday 29th November

Yes, a whole day later! What did I do yesterday? Wasted it, as so often. But sometimes I think that's what Life is: a time of uncertain length (well, no more than a century), most of it consumed in sleep and survival (eating etcetera) and trivialities (gossip etcetera). Significance? Boris influence?

Well, that wasn't a very promising start, was it? What I must tell you is that I had a vivid dream (I who never dream!) last night. Most of it had evaporated before I woke up, as usually happens with me now. But one image remained: Jennifer, smiling. I took that with me on my walk this morning. And some acquaintances similarly on exercise-walks waved to each other, and even shouted greetings; which was also cheerful!

By the way, Alice, have you noticed any change in me? My style – writing style? It seems to me that I have become more garrulous, long-winded. In the past I would have thought that regrettable, and tried to suppress the impulse. Certainly I always told my students that Brevity was to be cultivated.

Anyway (depart, garrulity!). It's been a sunny but chilly day (about 10 degrees). I had a brisk walk before lunch. And after reading my novel (I should say "*re*reading") – Virginia Woolf's *To the Lighthouse*, one of my favourites – and then playing some Bach, I'll go to bed. Does that sound tame and boring? Well, I must admit that Life does feel, as for so many of us now, rather constricted. How long before we are liberated? Though I'm one of those who doubts that we will *ever* be able to return to our old lives, our old ways – and that could be a very good thing! What do you think?

But I'm just chattering again, aren't I?

Hoping for news of Jennifer. Yes, that's why I'm so restless, edgy.

I send my love to you and your two Guests. How I look forward to seeing you, dear Alice, and meeting them!

P.S. I think I forgot completely to say that I *did* watch that hour-long programme about those Nova Scotia Murders that happened while we were playing Schubert's Quintet. Like a contrast between two extremes, Evil and Good! And it was so disturbing that I almost turned it off. I didn't recall that *so many* people had been killed. The worst multiple murder in Canadian history. And so many of the victims and their families could have been neighbors and friends of mine, if I hadn't migrated to Ontario, after college and after both my parents had died. Sometimes I used to think that I should have gone back, to Truro or near there, for holidays at least, and of course I surely would have done if I'd still had family there. But to see glimpses of that familiar country so close to Truro, and especially to hear the sadness and anger in the voices of family and friends of the victims – it was so very painful, Alice! And it just added to my worry about Jennifer. I guess I thought that somehow seeing that programme and learning more about the killings might mitigate my worrying, but it didn't. In fact, I think seeing all that made my worrying worse. What a painful time we're living through – sadness and worry all round us. And with COVID, so much suffering, so many deaths. But I said I wouldn't go on about that.

The telephone rang just as I was washing-up after Supper. Christopher! It was Christopher, and he had some news, *possibly* good news. They have made contact with a farmer who claims to have seen a woman walking ahead of a man along a path, in the distance but not very far from where the car was found. "How did she look, was she walking willingly, did the man seem to be threatening her?" – "I couldn't tell, it was too far away, I just had a glimpse." – "Do you think he saw you?" – "No, they were struggling through the snow and ice, it's quite a rough path" – So now tomorrow, Christopher said, they'll be going to all the farms near there they haven't visited so far, and checking again some of those that they visited earlier. And also all the buildings that house farm-workers. Oh, if only Jennifer's all right! Christopher said he'll email me immediately if he has news – or telephone his mother – and then *she* will telephone or email.

I *do* like Christopher. And his mother – Helen. I'll let you know immediately if there's news.

So now I'll go to bed feeling a bit more relaxed!

Alice: Sunday 29th November

It's quite late – almost midnight. So you'll be asleep and get this tomorrow.

All's well now – thanks to Dr Galbraith – but I have been very worried about Maria just lately – and I could see that Joseph was worried too. I thought it was probably morning-sickness. But what's happened now is that she was suddenly very sick this afternoon, when she was washing-up after lunch – I think I told you how she always insists on doing that. Well, no more – Dr Galbraith said *No more of that!*, after she'd examined Maria – Joseph and I had gotten her into bed, and that's where she'll have to stay for a while. I was worried, of course, that she might have been about to have a miscarriage, and I got the impression from Dr Galbraith that it may have been a near thing! But it looks as if she'll be all right, and Dr Galbraith said she'll be coming back tomorrow to see her – "No more nonsense – Joseph can do the washing-up and anything else that needs doing from now on" she said. I didn't say anything, but of course Joseph can't always be here, his hours aren't regular, and *I* can do all that, I always *have* done it!

So that's all for now, Anna. I'm so hoping for good news about Jenny.

Anna: Monday 30th November

Oh, now I feel guilty, Alice! When we were all in your and Boris's house for the Schubert Quintet, I didn't even think of helping you in the kitchen, most of the time! Oh, well – I am sinful, as my new religious meditation is exposing. I am so glad that Maria seems to be fine now. Please give her my love, and tell her I'm praying for her – and her baby. As for Jennifer, no news – but there's still time today. As you know, they're behind us timewise in the West, so maybe there'll be a message. I'm hoping and praying, as you are.

What a dreary, dreary day! Wintery rain, which the CBC says will probably change to SNOW this afternoon. It must be the same for you in Toronto. Ugh! Winter!

But Oh Anna, Anna, you of little faith! Joy, joy, joy! They have *found* her, Alice – she's safe, *she's safe*! Exhausted but safe. Helen, and then Christopher, telephoned to tell me. They said they'll email details when they have the chance – obviously the first priority is to make sure about her health etcetera. I asked if I could speak to her, but they said she was in hospital and asleep, and when she wakes they'll need to check her physically and mentally, but Christopher says she seems to be in a remarkably good state. And, Helen said, Christopher was actually the one who found her, and he carried her up from the basement where she'd been kept since the abductor got her to his farm, and he called for an ambulance from the nearest hospital, where she is now – And then

– Well, it's a long story, and complicated. I'm longing to talk to her and hear her voice, of course, but Helen said we'll have to be patient because she's gone through so much, and I do understand that. But I'm just so very grateful. And it's shown me, too, how insensitive and thoughtless I've been – When Jennifer suddenly told me that she would be going West with Ken, I was surprised, *shocked, offended* that she hadn't discussed that with me, and I suppose because I hadn't really noticed anything, because I was just enjoying what she gave me, her youthful enthusiasm and companionship, which I guess I'd come to expect and depend on – and she and Ken had obviously been more in touch by iPhone or email than I'd realized – And so then I behaved like James, with anger and, yes, also jealousy – But, sorry, Alice, I shouldn't be writing these things, they'll just embarrass you – And really they're irrelevant. Jennifer's safe, safe, safe. That's what matters. So put it down to relief!!! God is offering me a chance to redeem myself and make things right with Jennifer, I think. Please tell me if I have offended *you*, my dear Friend, and if so please forgive me.

So – That's the news of this day, Alice. My love to you and your Family. I'll write again soon.

Alice: Monday 30th November

Such a relief, Anna! I am so glad. Dear Jenny. And not seriously hurt by that terrible experience, it seems. After being abducted and so badly-treated and isolated. Of course we can't know the full story until she tells us what happened, or as much as she chooses to tell us. Did they say anything about the man who killed Ken and abducted her – who he is, and has he been caught, and what's going to happen to him? But I'm so glad that there seems to be such a happy ending. Except for poor Ken, of course. No doubt there'll be more information soon about it all – I guess the media will be after it, turn it into another of their melodramas – like that CBC programme you saw (I'm glad I didn't!) about those terrible murders in Nova Scotia that happened while we were playing the Schubert Quintet.

Good news about Maria, too – or at least *better* news. She says she's feeling fine now, ready to do the washing-up again! But I said *NO*, you must rest and get strong, for the baby's sake, and that's what the doctor said, that you must rest, so it's an *order*. And her husband looked sternly at her, he clearly agrees.

So all's well, for the moment at least. Though n*ot* in this province, or this country, as long as COVID rampages and people behave stupidly and don't take precautions!

And, Anna – I have nothing to forgive you for. You're a steady hand and a good companion. And don't forget, we have a lot in common, even blood – being related, however distantly. And we have music and our memories of Boris and the Quartet. What more could we want, or need?

THREE

Helen: Tuesday 1st December 2020
Dear Anna,

I hope you are keeping well. I have more good news and information for you, about Jennifer. Christopher says she is doing well, according to the Doctor (who apparently is highly-respected) and Noel (my husband) is on his way to the hospital to join up with Christopher and try to visit Jennifer, or talk to her Doctor if she is still too fragile to have any visitors.

I will telephone you or send another email if there is more news about her progress. What a truly dreadful experience she has gone through, poor girl, but I remember (she was much younger then, of course, and I was Noel's Secretary, as she may have told you) – I remember how greatly she impressed us with her beauty, charm and resilience. Although, as you know, Noel is her Uncle, they had never met before that, because he had been sent to Canada near the beginning of the War; and then, after both her parents were killed in an accident some time later (I hope I'm recalling correctly), Jennifer was brought up by one of her Father's Sisters (now deceased). There was no connection with us until she immigrated to Canada and became a music-teacher in Ontario, some years ago. You probably know that too!

I'll write again when I know more, after Noel visits her in the hospital. Our good wishes,

Helen

Anna: Tuesday 1st December

SNOW! WINTER WONDERLAND!!! When I opened my eyes this morning – there, bright in the sunshine, what a glorious vision! Of course it had been predicted, but the sudden change is still a shock, and, according to the CBC News later this morning, there have been so many crashes, fender-benders and worse, on the highways, and we were warned to stay indoors today if possible. No problem for me, of course – but for so many others, having to get to work, or help others and keep society running, the snow is a major difficulty. I hope you'll be safe and snug, Alice – and your Maria. How is she doing? I hope all is well with her.

I'm attaching the email that came during the night from Helen – who is the wife of Jennifer's Uncle Noel (I think I told you about him, and her and their son Christopher, who, thank goodness, found Jennifer – just in time probably). Helen's email leaves some questions, but it is good to know Jennifer is in hospital now and getting good medical attention after her ordeal – which must have been dreadful, truly dreadful, with poor Ken being shot to death in front of her, and then – well, so much we don't know yet. I'll reply to Helen's email right after this, Alice. And of course I'll let you know any other news.

Anna: Tuesday 1st December

Dear Helen, thank you so much for your email.

Poor Jennifer! I have been thinking and praying so much about her – if you get a chance, please give her my love, and Alice's (a close mutual friend). We are so grateful to you and your husband – and your son Christopher, who found her and was good enough to let me know – after he saw my email address on my many messages in her iphone, which the Police have.

I am so very grateful to you, Helen, and your husband and son, for all you have done. It will be lovely to meet you. Meanwhile, is there more you can tell us? Is Jennifer able to talk now about her ordeal: all that happened after they stopped and poor Ken was killed? Maybe she won't want to talk about it, or even recall it, until she feels back to normal? And of course that is the most important thing, that she should be happy and healthy again after such a traumatic ordeal.

Again, Helen, THANK YOU SO MUCH and please give our thanks to your husband and son.

Sincerely, Anna

Anna: Tuesday 1st December

Here I am again, Alice – back after replying to Helen's email that I forwarded to you.

Now, what was I going to say? The snow that is so beautiful on all the trees, it's falling off slowly (no wind), but it's still snowing very softly. And suddenly I was reminded of a poem I love, by Thomas Hardy, that I used to teach. It goes like this (I'll quote only a few lines of it, but the whole poem is delightful!): "Every branch big with it, / Bent every twig with it; / Every fork like a white web-foot; / Every street and pavement mute: / Some flakes have lost their way, and grope back upward, when / Meeting those meandering down they turn and descend again. / The palings are glued together like a wall, / And there is no waft of wind with the fleecy fall." I'm cheating, as you've probably guessed! Found the old Penguin that I once used in my English class. (My poetry shelf!) But I won't carry on quoting it now, though I'm tempted to. How I love this poem! Oh, I will – At the end, a sparrow "enters a tree" and "immediately / A snow-lump thrice his own slight size / Descends on him and showers his head and eyes, / And overturns him, / And near inurns him ..." But the poet's gentle humour here is itself overturned, and the poem ends by acknowledging suffering and even death, both of them averted but not eradicated: "The steps are a blanched slope, / Up which, with feeble hope, / A black cat comes, wide-eyed and thin; / And we take him in." Oh, I love that poem! It calms me, even while it acknowledges unhappiness and pain. And maybe that's also why it came to me this snowy morning: Jennifer's ordeal, the threat to her life, her suffering, her survival. One day I'll read this poem to her. And this poem has also made me think of another, which you know well, the one that Boris so often quoted, Browning's "Abt Vogler". "The C

Major of this life" etc! I'll read it again later!

But now, again. What is there to say while we wait for further news of Jennifer? Well, Alice – I'm thinking, as December starts, and as all the worry and concern about COVID just seems to increase and intensify (though mitigated a little by repeated hopeful references and predictions, as by PM Justin Trudeau earlier this morning, on CBC – Matt Galloway interviewing him on his programme "The Current") – I'm thinking that I must focus my thoughts on *gratitude* – gratitude for Jennifer's survival. Also, as I mentioned to you earlier (didn't I? I'm getting so forgetful), my own religious revival continues, and I have even unearthed a few of my religious books, which are again starting to influence me. Does the word COMPLINE mean anything to you? It's the final monastic service of the day, the one that completes the Christian monks' canonical hours. And for me, when I was very religious in my youth, and had a very religious boyfriend (who did in fact become a monk later!), reading that service aloud with him, in the evening, was rapturous! Well, I guess they didn't last for more than one semester, that relationship *or* the Compline readings; but now here they are again, offering to give me spiritual peace! So many lovely prayers! I remember especially "Be present, O merciful God, and protect us through the silent hours of this night, so that we, who are wearied by the changes and chances of this fleeting world, may repose upon thy eternal changelessness ..." Yes, I do remember it; must have been waiting all the years to return now? And now Jennifer – And maybe it has also been inspired by my hearing yesterday, on the CBC, an interview with Lisa Raitt, MP (or ex-MP?), about her managing, with impressive sensitivity and generosity, her husband's early-onset Alzheimer's. Very moving, and impressive.

But I'm sorry, Alice, if you're reading this – with growing impatience, no doubt, because you have so much more to do, that *needs* to be done, than I do. I'll come back down to reality. And yes, the deepening worry about the Second Wave of COVID now intensifying across Canada, and the USA, and many other countries around the world. (Canada: over 12,000 COVID deaths so far; Quebec, over 7,000 COVID deaths; Alberta, over 450 COVID hospitalizations; British Columbia, 46 COVID deaths, during the past weekend, its highest number; etcetera!). I can't keep up with all the numbers – scrawling them down, accurately or inaccurately – and so what? They mean that a terrible disease, a 'pestilence' that began less than a year ago in China, has seized the world, taken humanity by the throat, threatened destruction – and Way to Go, Humanity! – or maybe No Way to Go, but do we actually have a choice, individually or collectively? I wish Boris was still here – Hey, Boris, what do you think NOW? – "Sorrow is hard to bear, and doubt is slow to clear, / Each sufferer says his say, his scheme of the weal and woe: / But God has a few of us whom he whispers in the ear; / The rest may reason and welcome: 'tis we musicians know." Oh yes, Robert Browning? Do tell! "… my resting-place is found, / The C Major of this life: so, now I will try to sleep." Happy dreams, dear Boris. *I* must struggle on. – Oh, Alice, just count all this as nonsense – if you have even read this far. Self-indulgent nonsense. What has happened to me? Something has collapsed, deep within, and I am struggling to breathe, in my ruins; struggling to emerge into daylight – that's how it feels. A new woman who is an Old Woman (look at her wrinkles and greying hair!): the first woman silenced by self-doubt and insecurity, the second – oh, the second!

Again, please forgive me, Alice. Count all this ranting, if you have read it, as nonsense. And if I have offended you, forgive me. I am feeling very tense, longing to hear again from Helen.

Anna: Tuesday 1st December

And I *have* heard – but not from Helen. From *Noel*, and then from Christopher. Noel telephoned in the early evening: just a short conversation, mainly for him to say that Jennifer was now in a better state, and Christopher was at her bedside and would email me from the hospital; he's been told by the doctor that he shouldn't stay long, she needs as much rest as possible. Something in Noel's voice troubled me, but – well, I just had to wait.

Then, while I was eating my frugal supper, I somehow thought that Jennifer was trying to talk to me, and when I checked my iPhone, there *was* a message – from Christopher, a long one, and oh – Alice, here it is, I'm forwarding it, as before, with my reply. And as you'll see, it's not easy – if only one could talk to Jennifer, but that will obviously have to wait until she's fully recovered, and even then – well, we'll have to see *then*. Please let me know what you think.

Christopher: Tuesday 1st December

Dear Anna, I have just left Jennifer. She is recovering well, the doctor says, but she needs more rest. I'll probably go back to Vancouver soon – no need for me here now, to help in the investigation (if there ever was any need!), they've found the man who murdered Ken & abducted Jennifer. As I suspected, he was a local farmer who was thought by the farming-community to be very odd – a loner who had tried and failed to be a policeman before becoming a failed farmer – with a failed marriage. No children, thank God, or known relatives (they're still checking that). But what happened, exactly – after he killed

Ken & abducted Jen – well, we'll have to wait until Jen can give more information. But I was saying – he was found dead in a marshy area, other side of the farming community, almost certainly suicide & I think they've found the weapon. But Anna – it's mainly about Jen you are wanting to know, & I don't know how much I should tell you. Obviously I can't ask Jen, but you are her closest friend, aren't you, & I know you would always be very discreet, if you think that is necessary, I don't know if it is. Maybe I am being unnecessarily cautious. Anyway here it is – Jen is pregnant. They think they can save the baby, that's what I was told – in the hospital – I drove her there as fast as I could, she was in a bad way, battered & bleeding. When I broke down the door to the basement of the abductor's farm (I don't know his name, or didn't register it), she was lying on an old mattress, and I thought for a moment she was dead. – Anyway, Anna, I don't think you would really want all the details, & I hope you are keeping well. I am going to spend the night here at the hospital, near her. Dad couldn't stay but he brought me some fresh clothes (which I sure needed!). Maybe we'll be able to meet one day, when this COVID thing finally ends!? Good wishes from Christopher Wiseman.

Anna: Tuesday 1st December

So there it is, Alice. It seems as if Jennifer was fortunate to *survive*, doesn't it? And we don't know yet whether she has been severely affected by what she has gone through.

But of course what troubled me, apart from her fragile state, was Christopher telling me that she's pregnant. I had no idea! Of course the pregnancy wasn't extremely advanced, I assume, and I now think that it was probably with Ken, when we were at Boris's house, just after the Schubert Quintet, and that's why they decided to travel together to the West, where of course she has family and he may have had family or friends (I didn't really know him very well – but I always thought he was gay, mainly because of his relationship with James – but probably he was bisexual). And Jennifer went to James's Remembrance in Toronto in June, was it? and stayed with Ken for one or two nights (she went by bus, I didn't go – I'm not sure why – partly because of not really liking James, I guess, and also I thought there should have been a Remembrance for Boris and there hadn't been).

Anyway, I realize now that I should have gone. Maybe Jennifer thought it was because I didn't like James and Ken at all. And if so, that might have given her further cause to go West with Ken – in fact, *she* may have persuaded *him* to go on that journey. She was always very sympathetic and generous – sometimes to very unworthy people. (Like me!) *Mea culpa!* And she would surely have known she was pregnant by that time. And maybe that's another possible reason she wanted to go.

Now I'm going to bed, after reading the Compline service, and praying to behave more honestly and generously and lovingly. Like you do, dear Alice.

Alice: Tuesday 1st December

Thank you for your email and news about Jenny. You're *too hard on yourself*, Anna! You are a *great* friend to Jenny, and to me and others.

I think we're all of us wound up, and tense, what with the COVID shut-down, and we just have to endure that until the Vaccine is available – which will be in a few months, judging by what I hear. And that will be our Christmas Present! Getting impatient and tense won't help – in fact, it will make things worse, as the Medical Authorities are trying to say as loudly as possible. We still have a ways to go, and even when it's available, the vaccine will have to be delivered – and that will be complicated and take time, and seems that there's already a lot of quarrelling among countries and within populations about who will get it or who will get it first! So I say Be patient! Not that anybody's listening to little old me! Meanwhile frail elderly people are still dying in seniors' homes, and hospital staffs are hardly able to cope, and children aren't being educated or even loved, and restaurants are closing down! And that's the end of *my* sermon!

Maria is doing well, Anna. Dr Galbraith came again today, to take her temperature and declare her very much alive. I'm so sorry to hear there's a chance of Jenny losing the baby, but so glad to know she is in hospital being well-looked-after. Please give her my love when you can. That young man, Christopher, is a Hero, isn't he? Wouldn't it be loverly if they could all come here for Christmas? But I know that's just a dream. At least I'll have Maria and her husband and of course her baby by then, to love and cherish. And you? Can *you* come, Anna? That would be truly *loverly*. What does Hamilton have that Toronto hasn't? No, don't answer, you'll say "A Mountain" but that's a lie, it's only a little Escarpment. And a little Botanical Garden. And a few Waterfalls. And Nothing Else. Except an Inferiority Complex! Poor Hamilton!

See! I can be irresponsible and thoughtless even more than you! "Two old ladies, locked in a lavatory", do you know that one? But it should be "washroom", whatever the Queen says. Off with her head and GOOD NIGHT! And COME!

Christopher: Wednesday 2nd December

Hi there, Anna (I hope you don't mind me being so familiar, but I don't know your surname anyway!).

Just to tell you that Jen opened her eyes when I approached her this morning. She didn't talk –

But she did look at the world, which included me.

She has a lovely smile, I'm sure you'll agree, & she made ME smile. We both smiled!

Did you know, this is a secret, or WAS a secret before I told you, I am only a year younger than her.

Also, I LIKE MUSIC – not her sort of music, which I guess is your sort of music.

Also, I SING!!! Not your snotty Operatic singing, "Trala", but real music that real people like.

At least you like Leonard Cohen and HALLELLLLUJAH (have I spelt it right?).

So you do appreciate GREAT CANADIAN MUSIC even though you haven't (yet) heard me sing!

So, Anna – looks like maybe we've got a great future together, you & me.

BUT – it all depends on Sleepy Beauty, AKA Jen, who is truly beautiful & must be woken up.

With my kiss!

Then she did wake up, & smiled twice more when I sang her my latest love song.

"I love you, Sleepy Beauty, and YOU MUST LOVE ME."

That's enough for now, back to your lonely burrow, Kris (I don't like "Christopher", so GOODBYE).

Oh Ms Anna, forgive my tomfoolering.

If you'd asked my Daddy, he'd have said "That lad's got a hole for a head".

But if you'd asked my Ma, she'd have said "Yes, he's my son, but I wish he had more class".

So there we are. Aren't we?

P.S. She divorced Daddy & I hardly ever see her now. Helen's only Number Two Mummy.

Anna, she's FINE, she's BACK, and when I mentioned YOU, she smiled. I promise.

I think she'd like me to send you her love, and I obey! SHE SENDS YOU HER LOVE.

– I'm Chris, and I'm so happy!

Anna: Thursday 3rd December

Alice, what do you think of that? Is the lad mad? I haven't replied yet – shall I tell him to faff off? But you know, how does it go? about the blind leading the blind – No, "In the country of the blind, the half-blind man is king", something like that! What a surprise to find his email this morning! I laughed and laughed and laughed – and you know, I don't think any of us have laughed for so long!!! It almost hurt. All those unused muscles! If anyone can cheer Jennifer up, cure her of hurt, *he's* the one, I think. Do you agree? But it's uncertain still – everything's uncertain. But at least she's smiling. We just have to go forward, with optimism and determination. When I reply to Chris, I'll invite him into our conversation, if you agree? Anyway, he's probably seen all the emails I sent to Jennifer when she was travelling West – all the emails that *she* hasn't seen yet. Oh, Alice –

I've even been forgetting to *paragraph* this effusion. Must have been an effect of the Kris Onslaught! I wonder what his music is like; it does sound as if he actually composes some of the songs that he sings – unless "I love you, Sleepy Head" is just a joke. Well, *I'll* put it to music, and accompany myself on my violin. How about that? I should be creative! I *must* be creative!

Yes, *enough* – you'll be thinking I'm off my rocker (that's an expression I've picked up from Jennifer, she has some choice English sayings and swear-words! If you pull her hair.). So I'll stop.

I fear that the CBC News will present further COVID gloom, but of course one must know what's happening, or not happening, and try to do what we can to help – so many, especially Seniors, suffering.

Over and Out.

Anna: Thursday 3rd December

Hullo, Krissie, aka Cheekyhead (a name my Mum used to call me when I was a cute but disobedient little girl – I don't see why it shouldn't be bisexual?) – Thank you for your Effusion!!! I must confess that it amused and entertained me – you have a domineering way with words which I guess extends to your musical effusions? So I will look forward to hearing one of those, the wildly-popular but infamous "I love you, Sleepyhead": can you send me a recording of it via your iPhone if possible (I am ignorant about contemporary technology, and once, not so long ago – well, that story can wait for when we meet, as I hope will happen before long. Your parents have been so kind to me, and of course, even more, to Jennifer, and surely I will have an opportunity to express my gratitude to them in person eventually).

Oh – Jennifer, Jennifer, Jennifer! What a joy to know she is safe and recovering. And that you are there for her, Christopher. Are you a Graduate Student? If so, maybe that's why you can give time and consideration to her, and stay near her as she recovers. We are so grateful, Alice and I (Alice is Jennifer's friend as well as mine, living in Toronto), to know that you are there beside her as she recuperates. Maybe I shouldn't ask this, but will she be able to be with your parents and you in Vancouver when she's fit to leave the hospital? You know, it's – After all the worry, it's wonderful, truly wonderful, that she has you beside her, giving love and support. We thank you so very much!

I think, too, that my rather crazed behavior since getting your last email expresses great RELIEF. I would like to think so, anyway. Please forgive or ignore it, whichever is easiest! I think I am coming back to my senses.

Our grateful good wishes – Anna

Christopher: Thursday 3rd December

Dear Anna (if I may, but you have set a bad example) – I am replying immediately, in some alarm – NO, DON'T GO BACK TO BEING STAID & DISCREET, you're *much better than that* – & younger! The world wants you as you are, not as you *were*. You are open, friendly, lovable and FUN! I don't have anything but my bad behavior to keep your attention – and we WANT THAT, me & your lovely young friend – Who is recovering very fast, ask the doctor & nurses, & who SMILES more & more. (Of course my jokes split her sides, which is cause for some alarm to the medical staff here, but so far no bad consequence.) You asked, in a somewhat rude way, about my singing & songwriting, so be warned that ear-mufflers are the thing when I get going – & I often do. Yes, I play the guitar & SING my own songs, audiences have been known to run screaming but since you have had the temerity to ask you must be ready to SUFFER when we meet. Which will happen in the New Year, I predict. 2021!!! We'll throw a party together in honour of our Princess. And the Destruction of COVID! Yes, I am crazy like *you*, Old Lady. – Kris

Alice: Thursday 3rd December

So I'm the staid one, am I? Is that what your newfound girlhood implies? Well, *I* have responsibilies, like looking-after a sick young woman while *you* send mad love-notes to a boy half your age (half? more like quarter!). Oh, Anna, what a

135

crazy world we live in now!

I hear this morning (yes, I am listening to the CBC now too) that the Brits have beaten the world to a Vaccine for COVID, which if true is very good news (God loves the Brits?), but meanwhile there were 727 new cases of COVID here in Toronto over the weekend, and the Virus is spreading fast and furious in countries round the world. Death, sickness, and worry, worry – the story of our times. But the sun is shining and snow still clings to trees – it's a lovely breezy chilly day!

Maria is still doing well. Dr Galbraith told me, as she left after her last visit, that she's confident all should go well and the baby could arrive in a few weeks.

I'm hoping you will join us for Christmas, Anna! Even if illegally. Surely you can commit yourself now? Provisionally, at least. Then Maria will have two supporters as well as her husband in attendance, and of course angelic Dr Galbraith, who has made it clear that she expects me to telephone her the moment Maria's labour begins. She is such a good patient, and always so appreciative – like her husband, who is clearly such a good worker – when I telephoned his workplace recently to check on something or other, his boss answered the phone and took the opportunity to tell me how much his work is valued. We must make sure that our two refugees – three – are welcomed into Canada! And we will: there is no way we would ever allow anything else, is there?

Helen: Thursday 3nd December
Dear Anna,

Here I am, still with flour on my hands! Yes, I'm starting to cook for Christmas, I always make a Christmas Cake, something I learnt from my Mother when I was a girl, and the

Boys (I always call Noel and Christopher that!) love it and *demand* it! But I have been talking to Chris, he calls me most nights when he's away. Rather late tonight (that's why I'm emailing rather than calling you – though as I write that I remember, too late, that you're a few hours behind us!), Chris was with Jen in the hospital for a quite a long time, he said, talking with her, when she was awake (he says she is awake for longer periods now but it's unpredictable). And he said he was a bit worried by her talk, and emotions, she was weeping at times. And he thought it was mostly about the man who abducted her (she doesn't know he's dead – drowned in a lake a few kilometers away, Chris said, but she apparently thinks he's alive and on the run still – and, I don't understand this, she has sympathy for him – perhaps it's a delusion). Of course she must have been terrified all the time she was his prisoner. His name was John, apparently. He stole a vehicle, and when it was running out of gas, he abandoned and concealed it, and waved down the car Jen was in.

Chris spoke privately to the doctor, before he left to go back to the farm nearby, where he's staying until we can get to you, Noel's in meetings with the Premier and Ministers until the end of this week – But the doctor thought it was very good that Jen was talking and he told Chris not to worry, just be natural with her and always try to convey cheerful feelings. (Sorry if I'm being long-winded, but my husband says I don't always explain things fully.)

Of course I don't want to worry you, and you shouldn't be worried. It's just that she seems to be obsessed with the man, the abductor, Chris says, and how should he handle that? Is it destructive to her recovery, or is her mind just having to deal with painful memories? At first Chris thought she might be trying to deal with sexual abuse or worse – you know, the man attempting to rape her? But he decided it wasn't that, because Jen wasn't angry, she was just sad, he said, "so sad". But she also smiled sometimes. So he was puzzled. Why wouldn't she feel *angry* now? "She isn't one for self-pity" I remember Chris said. I think basically he was not only puzzled, but disturbed.

Did you know, did she ever say to you, that she left us earlier very suddenly – when she first visited us, I mean, some years ago? And Chris thought that – this gets difficult, and maybe I shouldn't – but now Chris says it may be a factor, and important or even crucial for her recovery, he said – though he tends to exaggerate sometimes. You see, Noel had visited Jen, with Chris, when they first contacted us, the RCMP, and told us what had happened and she was in hospital, they got our telephone number and address from her iPhone, I think – And when she opened her eyes and saw Noel, Chris says she seemed somehow tense and *frightened* and closed her eyes again, and seemed almost to be trying to turn away.

Now – I'm telling you all this in confidence, Anna (is that right, 'Anna'? I think so, but when I'm upset I tend to forget things). And of course we're *all* worried about Jen.

Did you know I met her first when I was Noel's Secretary all those years ago, before his first wife ran off and he married me? I can still remember her as she was then, so *young* and *fresh* and – very *naïve*. Of course she was still new in Canada, a 'recent immigrant', as they say, or used to – maybe you can't say 'recent immigrant' now, like so many other things you can't say these days. Anyway, to cut a long story short, as I think they still say – or some people do! She seemed very happy with us for a while, she and Chris, who is a bit younger than her – he's Noel's son by his first wife, you probably guessed that – the two of them got on so well, laughing and chattering together – and he enjoyed showing her Vancouver and the Island, and taking her to concerts – not *my* type of concert, or yours probably, but she clearly enjoyed them – after all she was a young music-teacher! – and Chris was already singing and composing and getting quite popular. Noel and I were getting married that summer, he had already proposed to me, the guest-lists were being decided – and Noel was respected by the Premier, who often asked him for advice, some people even wondered if he would go into politics himself, there was a lot of talk about that – But I'm rambling again, as Chris would say! To resume, then: suddenly there was – well, she seemed to think that Noel had actually tried to *rape* her. Of course I tried to calm her down and convince her she was imagining things – as she *was!* Noel of course denied what she said, he has always denied it, and I know him well enough, *more* than well enough, to know he was telling the truth – and it was all hushed up – for *her* sake. And she left after that, even before the Wedding, in the middle of the night if I remember correctly, and didn't even send Congratulations. And after that we didn't hear a thing from her until – well, until we had that telephone call from the Police to say she was in hospital and had been attacked and abducted. But they didn't say she was pregnant. In fact, the baby may be due quite soon, from what Chris told me. And he said we *must* help her – he's like his Father, always seeing the best in everybody – and he set off immediately, even before I could contact Noel and discuss it all with him. But then Noel said that we could fly there for just a day, between his meetings, and then maybe we could heal the past and find reconciliation, those were his words. He is so kind and generous, and Chris is just like him.

So that's how things are. Noel even said maybe we can

bring Jen here for Christmas and New Year's, he's so kind and generous and forgiving, and of course she *is* his niece, his only remaining relative since the deaths of his sister and brother-in-law in a car-accident – and the death of that cousin of his who was a famous cellist and looked after Jen after her parents were killed. Did you know, of course you wouldn't – that Noel was sent to Canada after the War began, his father had an "old chum" he called him, who had emigrated to British Columbia, and he said he would be glad to have Noel as he and his wife had no children. But I'm talking (writing!) too much again.

It would be lovely to meet you. Chris tells me that you are a very close friend, and fellow-teacher, of Jen in Hamilton (I don't know Hamilton, although once we passed by it, if I remember correctly, after visiting Niagara Falls – Noel was at a Conference in Toronto).

If Jen comes to us for Christmas – Chris says he could drive her, I guess she'll be very heavily pregnant by then – and why don't *you* come too, Noel could probably arrange that, even if the dreaded COVID pandemic is still raging! – though it seems, with the news of the Brits having beaten the rest of the world to a Vaccine, we will all be free of COVID soon!

With best wishes from Noel, Christopher and Helen

Christopher: Thursday 3rd December

Hi there, Goldilocks! My Mater has told me she has sent you one of her Endless Email Epistles (remember, she was once Dad's Private Secretary!). So now I will Compensate, & save your time & be BRIEF. Just to tell you that this morning Jen opened her eyes, looked hard at me, and SMILED!!! Again. I took one of her hands & we held hands forever. BOTH SMILING! And she told me her weeping *had* actually been for the man who abducted her ("he wasn't a bad man, Chris, he didn't hurt me & he could have"). So – all is very well & YOU ARE INVITED TO THE WEDDING – next Spring, front row! – Big Bad Kris

Anna: Thursday 3rd December
Alice, I've received a long long long email from Chris's mother, Helen. Would you like me to copy it to you as usual? It's mostly about Jennifer and her relationship with Crazy Chris's family. (He has emailed me too!) Yes, I know you are very busy, looking after Maria and so on. But my Feminine Instinct tells me that CC *is* truly and madly, more than he even knows himself, *in love with Jennifer* – they knew each other well for a while in BC some years ago. Every time she smiles, his heart goes BOOMPITY BOOM (do you remember that silly song? Sophia Loren and who-was-it, that British comedian film-star whose name escapes me). Of course the pregnancy-thing may be a problem – if she doesn't lose the baby, which must be due before long – I pray and pray that she will have a safe delivery – and these days, well, they be-have differently, this generation, from the ways of an old Coot like me (no, I didn't actually include you!). So WE'LL SEE!

And meanwhile I wanted to tell you that, after long and careful thought about all possible fictional facts and fallacies and the hopefully-trumpless Fateful Future, I HAVE DECID-ED TO ACCEPT YOUR INVITATION FOR CHRISTMAS! (And New Year's?) In fact, let me know when it might be helpful for you to have my ever-helpful presence. And I'll be there, quite pronto, with my newly-refurbished (but masked) SMILE! Jennifer and I both SMILE! Frequently! Radiantly! IF I can smuggle myself over to you – Are you ready for Illegal?

Did you know that she – Well, there's so much of interest

141

in Helen's email that I WILL forward it to you so you will have some light reading. While waiting to be jabbed with the Vaccine that, according to the latest News, "will soon roll out", and it seems possible that Old Ladies like you and me will qualify for it, top of the line-up! – though I sometimes wonder (don't read this!) why *our* lives, almost done anyway, should be considered worth saving, as much as those of children, and ahead of the young and active? And pregnant. We can debate this and other issues – it will entertain us while we toil in your well-appointed Kitchen. Oh, Alice, I can't wait to see you. If only Jennifer – but it's clear that Nasty Noel and family are going to claim her. They have regional as well as temporal priority!

What other news today? Increasing numbers of COVID infections and deaths here (but so far Hamilton isn't included in your Lockdown). And field-hospitals and military are to be "engaged in the fight against COVID in Alberta"; and BC has nearly 2,000 "active COVID cases" and 57 outbreaks in Seniors' homes, and the U.S. has recorded over 2,000 COVID deaths, so far! – etcetera, etcetera. I do understand, don't you, why 'COVID fatigue' is spreading everywhere. And 'COVID fear'! But it's also clear that we must just endure all this for a good while yet; there's no other choice. Our new life!

Oh, Alice, my love to you and to Maria and Joseph and the baby she's carrying. Oh, Jennifer, if only I could be with you right now! And not forgetting that handsome young Lord of Misrule – Oh, Christopher! You would love him too, Alice!

And P.S.

A Compline prayer for Advent: "Come, O Lord: and visit us in peace; that we may joy before thee with a perfect heart." (Or, in my case, a very *im*perfect heart.) (But I *do* "joy"!) (We should all do joy.)

And I'll end with the Compline prayer that I now try to pray every night as I get into bed: "The Lord Almighty grant us a quiet night and a perfect end."

I've been admitting to myself that I haven't cared enough about all the suffering and death caused, around the world, by the COVID Pandemic. Maybe I don't *recognize* enough, or *accept enough*, all the pain being experienced by so many. *We live in a world of such impossible beauty and terror*, as Boris once said to me (I've never forgotten the expression on his face when he said that). Yes, an infinite multitude of us creatures – human, animal, vegetable – And we must do all we can to alleviate pain, including the pain of our abused environment. So – But I am not a Priest, I merely gabble craziness, and I have long ago overstayed my welcome, if I ever *was* welcome? I must stop. I do stop.

YES BUT AND

Anna, CBC, SOTS, MM, CBC: Friday 6th December

I woke up this morning, turned on my little bedside radio, and – Cheerful chatter! Christmas music! It was the CBC's Annual MetroMusic Sounds of the Season Fundraiser for Toronto Foodbanks (which are now so much in demand and under increasing pressure in this COVID-dominated Season of joy and goodwill). They had already raised over $2,000! I listened lazily for half-an-hour, but now I'm up and about: watch out, world! And I dedicate this Very Final email to you, Alice – and you, Jennifer – and you, Kristopher – my Three Wise Humans (well, I can't say Wise *Men* when two of you are Women – and

Yes, I MUST GO. Let Us Now Go. As Gogo, or was it

Didi, said – sick of *Waiting for Godot*. And said. And said. And said. It's the Human Condition! Now, Old Woman: GO! GO!! GO!!!

Anna: Saturday 7th December

To all of you! After telephonic communications last night from Christopher and Helen, I know that Jennifer definitely can't be here in Ontario, with Alice and me, for Christmas (though I hope to hear from her before then!). Of course I know that her recovery from all she has suffered will likely be slow, and there is also the baby she is carrying – So it would be risky for her to travel to Toronto; much better to be in Vancouver with her family – Noel, Helen and Christopher. But I miss her; how I long to see her! So please tell her, Chris, we send her our deepest love – Alice, and me, Anna. And our very best wishes for her baby's safe, healthy birth.

I should tell you, also, that I am closing down this Communications Center when I leave here!

I will be travelling to Toronto on Monday next (9th Dec) to spend Christmas and New Year's with Alice and her Family (Maria, Joseph, and the child who will also be born soon). (*Two* babies on the way!) It's very kind of Alice to invite me, and of course I will make myself as useful as possible! If I escape Official Incarceration, and of course I will be heavily masked (I'm practising that – nurses do it, doctors do it, soon babies in their cradles will be doing it!). I'll take my violin, and maybe perform some Bach in Celebration, and in memory of Boris, James and Ken (our Three Wise Men, so deeply missed by Three Wise Women – Alice, Jennifer and me). (And I have just remembered Angela, who was so kind to me, how could I forget that for a moment? My love and gratitude, Angela!) (And thank you, God, for the gift of not one but three or more vaccines.)

Which reminds me (I can't think why) of a little Joke I specially created for you, Chros Chris. (Everyone else, close your eyes!) Three Wise Men got locked in a lavatory! *Who* rescued them, *who* let them out? *One Old Lady.* (All right, you can open your eyes now.) (And tell me it wasn't funny. But I don't care! I am *free* now, after so many years of nervous self-consciousness! In fact, at last I'm READY TO GO!!!) And so – dear Friends,

Merry Christmas, and may the New Year 2021 give us good health, stimulate good thoughts, encourage good loving generous behavior, and JOY, JOY, JOY.

Anna (yes, I'm krazy)

LOCKDOWN

ONE

Christopher: Tuesday 8th December

Hi, Grandmama! Yes, I know you signed off yesterday &
have probably already decamped to Toronto for imminent
arrest. (Actually, I hope not, for the Good Reputation of my
Family, which of course means Daddy's Reputation & that
of the Provincial Government he serves intermittently – If
you ask, I'll tell you more about that, & the flaming rows he
& I frequently have over their Apology for Decent Policy –
When there is so much suffering by the Poor, & so much
financial plundering by the Rich – Do you want one of my
speeches, no? My Stepmother smiles, desperately, when her
two most immediate Loved Ones dispute Government Policy at the dinner-table. "Let's not become too heated, dear."
"No, darling, I don't think he really meant that, did you,
dear?" Yes, Trump is going going going but will never be
Gone. Daddy, he represents Corporate America Today, and
he is not a Loser – Oh, Chris, shut up, you embarrassing ig-
noramus!) Oh, how did that happen? You're a bad influence
on me, Old Lady Anna. What's your surname, you must
have one. Desist! I am a naturally gentle soul, everyone
knows that.

But the Brits seem to have got ahead of the Herd, even
while teetering on the very edge of Common Market Doom.
May their Oxford medication abolish COVID! I do mean
that, Anna Anonymous. You will be near the front of the vac-
cine-receivers line-up, & I will be almost the last? But – I do
think we will be very fortunate, as a species, to scramble

through into freedom and sunlight. Then society will resume & audiences will again lavish attention on my musical ditties. After responding urgently to Global Warming, Third World Starvation, Animal Suffering etc. Surely?

Oh Anna. Sorry to be always the Fool, I am serious underneath, & I have more good news about Our Jennifer. She is recovering fast & faster! Was sat up for lunch today, by the masked nurses (we all must wear masks in the hospital, of course, & in any public places, as I guess you do in Ontario – I hate it, but of course it's for the public good & protecting the elderly from COVID) & Jen charms all the nurses, & even her gruff doctor, & me. We held hands again, & smiled at each other, & if it wasn't forbidden by our masks we would have kissed, I would have demanded that as partial payment for saving her from the murderous Monster. My one & only heroic act so far! The Princess should always be saved by a Prince! Then she should say Thank you. I love you.

Anna, I should be serious. This might be my last connection with you for a while, since you're about to shift yourself (or have done already) from Hamilton to your Friend in Toronto. In fact, I should do as you have already done & hereby hope that you & all around you will have a MERRY CHRISTMAS & a HAPPY HEALTHY NEW YEAR! I wish we could meet in the flesh – it's sad that you will be in Toronto (even if with friends) while Jen will be in Vancouver with me & my family. But one day I know we *will* meet. A great day that will be! Have you ever seen any of that CBC series "Still Standing", with an ebullient young host who travels Canada giving joyful recognition to small local communities? I'd love to do something like that – singing songs & making friends all round Canada! Dream on, Kris.

Well, that leads me back to your/my/our lovely Jennifer.

Please know, Anna, that I will always love her. If *she* feels like that towards *me*, we will be married as soon as possible, & her baby will be *our* baby, in the Spring of 2021. Whatever my Father & Stepmother may say, it *will happen!*

Anna's Diary: Thursday 10th December
So, here you are, Anna. In Toronto. With dear Alice.

Well, not *exactly*, at this moment, on what (judging by the bright sunlight pouring in through the window this morning) is a fine mild Winter day, just two weeks before Christmas. I've been here almost three days now: left Hamilton on Tuesday 8th, had an easy drive here along the highway, and no problem getting to Boris's house (I'll always call it that, I guess, even though he's no longer here); I parked beside Alice's car and was welcomed by her. I had put on my mask, but she hugged me tight as I got out of the car, and kissed my cheek, and said "Welcome, welcome, let me help you with your luggage" and soon we were sitting in the kitchen drinking tea and catching-up; and especially talking about poor Ken's horrible death and Jennifer's situation. I told Alice all I could, repeating all the details in emails, including about Christopher and his family; and also that, sadly for us, Jennifer (when she's well enough to leave the hospital) will be going to Vancouver for Christmas and New Year's (her Uncle Noel says he will fly her there in his private plane; he's a rich businessman). I told Alice all I knew about him; and about Krazy Kris his son; but without saying, I don't know why, that he wants to marry Jennifer because he was the one who rescued her! And loves her.

And what else? I helped Alice to make a Christmas Cake and cookies yesterday (she had the ingredients already, and of course I am a Super-Cook). I didn't get to meet the Refugee

Family who Alice is looking after while Maria, the pregnant young wife, who apparently is quite ill, has to stay in bed. Boris's Doctor (her name's Gilbert, if I remember correctly) visits regularly, Alice said, because Maria is frail. She and her husband are Refugees; he has work now through some relatives, if I remember correctly. So that's how things are. Of course, I won't be able to meet them for a while, so as to be sure there's no chance I could infect them with COVID.

That reminds me to record that a Vaccine to protect against COVID is about to become available in Canada, and has already been administered in the U.K. to a very elderly English woman who is now in all the news, famous in her wheelchair! What would you think about that, Boris! Of course there is a lot of speculation and chatter about it in the CBC News and Commentary programmes. Meanwhile, over 3,000 Americans died of COVID yesterday: a horrific result of Trump's earlier refusal even to admit the existence of COVID in the USA, and take measures against it. Oh, oh. He has done so much damage.

Now I'd better rise and shine! Like the sun. "Busy old fool, unruly sun!" I do think I am blest to be here, with Alice, while the second wave of COVID is breaking all around us. So much uncertainty about COVID still, too; and especially troubling in that its transmission is to an extent unpredictable; for instance, can children transmit it while being apparently untouched by it? (I do hope that, unlike that African disease, Bilharzia is it called, it doesn't get deep inside you and attack long afterwards?) Anyway, there's this Vaccine, about to be delivered and soon to be administered, to give us all some hope. So many are working to make it available, and waiting to administer it, that anticipation of rapid delivery is high: a Christmas Gift for all? One comment in the News this morning pointed out that it's only a year since COVID began in China and set off to attack the rest of the world! Only a year. But of course there's still uncertainty; and doctors and nurses, all medical staff, are exhausted and close to collapse.

But now – Up, up, up, Anna! I can hear Alice in the kitchen, I think.

After lunch.

Alice has gone off shopping, and I am in charge! If Maria calls, I am to put on my mask and go to her assistance: help her to the bathroom, bring her water, whatever. Her husband will be back later this afternoon, or this evening. Up to now, Alice has been able to shop only when he is here: which is clearly somewhat unpredictable. "And sometimes the line-up at the supermarket is long and slow" she said. "It's one way to meet and gossip with the neighbours, let's be positive, but difficult with masks so it quickly becomes a waste of time." Anyway, I am at least being of some use. When she gets back, I'll go for a walk, just in the neighbourhood. I remember that Ken and Jennifer would do that, the week we rehearsed and performed Schubert's Quintet. Oh, poor poor Ken: that was such a horrible thing to happen to him, shot and killed as he got out of his car thinking he was going to give help to a stranded driver; and then the man he was offering to help *killed* him and stole his car and drove off with Jennifer inside – she must have been stunned, terrified. Why do you allow that sort of evil act to happen, God? Boris and I want to know. We *demand* to know. We want to understand. Maybe Boris *does* know now.

And I am reading (or soon will be) T.S. Eliot's *Four Quartets* and other poems by that great poet. I remember when I was at University – not the best student, but I *did* try, and I did enjoy my EngLit classes with that elderly – oh yes, I can still see him, Prof Whatsisname, with his shaggy beard and fuggy glasses, and we would try not to snigger at his sagging pants (trousers?) and ancient jacket. But he had a lovely resonant voice. And Welsh accent, I think. And he would stand there, swaying and declaiming Eliot. Oh, and now I remember one of his favourite Eliot poems, it was *Journey of the Magi*, which began "A cold coming we had of it, / Just the worst time of the year / For a journey – " Well, I'm surprised I can remember even that much of it. But I noticed last time I was here, when we were rehearsing the Quintet – I looked at the books in Boris's bookcase, hoping for something light to read, maybe an Agatha Christie, and did notice he had several poetry-books (apart from Robert Browning's *Collected Poetry*, which was naturally sacrosanct because it contained "the C Major of this life" etcetera: the reverenced "Abt Vogler" poem). And yes, I have found Boris's copies of Eliot's *Collected Poems* and *Four Quartets* (which I have never read – the *Quartets* I mean). Thank you, Boris! I will start reading them tonight – I've just heard Alice's car – I think. Yes! So now I will be helpful bringing in her bags full of provisions to sustain us. Oh, Kros Kris, if you could see me now, about to rise and offer valued assistance – what have *you* ever done – apart from saving Jennifer's life? And falling in love with her.

Just re-reading the above diary entries, it suddenly struck me, *mea culpa*, that I have not offered to pay my share of accommodation costs here, especially for food (which COVID is making more and more expensive). I must remember to do that. But meanwhile, Alice is cooking our supper (Maria of course is most used to Eastern cooking, so Alice accommodates that with hummus and noodles and pita etcetera). Yes, I will read some Eliot. "Time present and time past / Are both perhaps present in time future, / And time future contained in time past." Oh. Not the best beginning, TSE. For me, anyway. Sounds as if Time is a bit confused, and certainly not acting like an arrow, as I thought was its nature. Like a pretzel? Why do I think that? Oh, now I think I can see what TSE was getting at. Obviously my brain is stale. I'll start serious TSE-reading tonight in bed. Another quotation just came into my head, but I don't know where it comes from, just that it's by TSE: "Old men ought to be explorers" but how does it go on? "Old women can stay at home and cook in the kitchen"?

Time for me to email our Lord of Misrule. No doubt he has been sitting anxiously at his laptop, waiting for my golden words! Alice seemed a bit amused about my relationship with him, though she didn't say anything disparaging. Of course she can't know, and I can hardly know myself, how important he has been, how he has liberated me from all my negative hesitancy! I am even starting to ask myself if I'm too old to be a Writer – my old brain seems to seethe with ideas and opinions! Maybe I don't need Agatha Christie. Maybe I need to write like Jane Austen (whom I have admired so greatly for so long!).

Anna: Friday 11th December
Hail to thee, Blithe Spirit!

I hope all is well with you, Chris. And also with Jennifer. I have been thinking and praying for you both. And now I am very happily installed in Boris's house, with Alice – and her two refugee guests, Maria and her husband: she's expecting a baby at almost any minute, and he is working for (I think) a cousin. There was no difficulty getting here from Hamilton, and our weather has been mostly quite mild and sunny for the time of year. I hope you are having good weather too? Christmas is so close now!

Well, no response yet – some hours later. In fact, I'll soon be off to bed. Alice seemed a bit weary and disconsolate, so I told her to go off to bed and I'd do the washing-up and see to tidying the kitchen (she is very messy, and never closes a drawer or cupboard, so I have to be careful not to injure my-self!). She and I ate in the kitchen, well apart from Maria and her husband (who arrived at about 5 o'clock: of course, now it's dark by then). We could hear them conversing in their own language (Arabic?). I'd love to play some Bach, and they might enjoy that – but then I thought I shouldn't cause any distraction. So, instead, I got into my laptop, for this chatter (as I will call these bits of diary, now that I'm trying to keep a fairly regular record – this *is* an exceptional time, after all). And I forgot to say that I went on a walk after lunch, just in the neighbourhood, "the immediate vicinity" as they say. How quiet and almost-deserted these streets are now!

It's a strangely contradictory time, I think. COVID still rampant, but there are warnings not to assume that the vac-cine, now soon to be available for administering to segments of the population (to hospital staff – doctors and nurses are so close to exhaustion now; to elderly people over eighty; etcet-era), will be some sort of magic cure. (And what about the anti-vaxxers, convinced that the vaccine will harm, even kill, them?) Meanwhile, the rates of COVID infection and death are in-creasing explosively in many countries around the world – in-cluding of course the USA, with over 100,000 Americans in hospital, nearly 300,000 deaths and a daily death toll of 3,000. In Canada, nearly 13,000 have died so far, and some provinces (like Alberta) have greatly-increased infection-rates.

I'm not good at keeping an accurate regular record. But I think we all need to know how vulnerable we are to COVID, especially the old and poor and essential-workers like nurses; and we all must do what we can to stop its spread. Looks as if it will be a long dreary housebound winter!

I have also been thinking of Alice's little refugee family and how especially hard they must be finding their lives here. I saw an article yesterday, in one of the newspapers Alice takes ("to keep up with the news" she said; she doesn't listen to the CBC as I do): it was about how the COVID Lockdown of Toronto feels like "something similar to war" for many Syrian refugees (over 45,000 have been resettled in Canada recently): "Streets are suddenly empty, stores shut down" – so it was just like being back in the bombed broken cities from which they had fled; and the wearing of masks has especially disturbed Syrians who fled "attacks with chemical weapons". Also – their first Winter here! The challenges they face are great, I feel proud of Alice for giving a home and protection to Maria as she comes close to the delivery of her child. (Alice said the baby is due, according to Dr Gilbert, quite soon now.)

Which again makes me think of Jennifer; is she still bed-ridden, or recovered enough to be on her feet? And Christopher. Silence! I'll send another email to him imminently – demanding an immediate response! I gave him Alice's telephone number, which I should have told him earlier, for urgent news – I just never thought of that before, I thought he would email, but maybe he's had to be with Jennifer, or maybe wanting to *talk* to me. Anyway, surely he'll telephone or email tomorrow.

Anna: Saturday 12th December

Chilly grey day! Why do I always start my daily record by noting the weather? Habit, no doubt.

Still nothing from Chris. I'm starting to get seriously worried. But no point in that, Anna! You have always worried too much; I can see (now) how Boris took advantage of that weakness in my character, and

Oh, oh, a telephone call – and Alice is calling me –

And it *was* Chris, but not with good news: in fact, I'm very troubled: Jennifer has lost her baby. He was also annoyed with me: "Why didn't you send me your friend's telephone number earlier? I need to talk to you" and then he told me about Jennifer's loss of her baby, and how he had been with her constantly. "She was so upset that I was really worried about her doing something extreme. But she's all right now, I think, talking more calmly and just needing company and encouragement, I think. I'll email you now, as soon as I can, and give you more details. I must go back to her: the Doctor and nurses are with her, but they'll be going soon. The Doctor said they think it really does help her to have me there, she had said so. And before that, before she – when I mentioned you, and your concern for her, she said 'Please tell Anna I'll be all right now and thank her for her prayers, they helped me, and for all the happy memories, the Schubert Quintet –' I apologized to him and said that I'll look forward to an email when he has the time – and after he's had a good sleep; which I could hear in his voice he badly needs. He was severe and serious; I had never heard that from him before.

I gave Alice a quick summary because she was just off to shop for food etcetera. "Oh, I'm so sorry that she lost the baby after all" Alice said. "Poor Jennifer! Ask that young man,

Christopher, to give her my love, please. Though, like you, I never had children, of course – well, any woman knows what it is to lose a child."

Now I'm writing late at night. Just quickly because I'm exhausted.

A day of shocks! Well, Jennifer's loss of her baby wasn't really a shock, because it was half-expected, or I should say *half-feared*. But the arrival of John (another John!) was certainly a surprise and a shock, and how it'll work out I don't know!

I had taken Maria some tea (I was masked, of course!) and helped her to and from the bathroom – she is looking really *very* pregnant now, and Dr Galbraith has told Alice that the baby could arrive very soon. Then I was making supper (mainly a hummus dish for Maria, and fish and chips for Alice and me!) when suddenly Alice came into the kitchen with a big bag of provisions and, right behind her, there was a shadowy figure (it gets dark earlier now): a man in shabby clothes, carrying another bag of provisions; and breathing heavily. He just stood there, after I took the bag from him, and looked at me with bleary eyes (he's Black, young I think, maybe early twenties, and seemed exhausted). Alice looked sharply at me (I could see she expected my shock) and said "Anna, this is John, he's going to be staying here tonight, in the basement, he needs a place to stay", and as I opened my mouth, she said firmly "Just for one night, and he needs something to eat and a bath and clean clothes – thank goodness I didn't give all Boris's clothes to the Sally Ann – and you've made a meal, and seen to Maria? – Thank you."

Later, when John was in a hot shower (luxuriating, no doubt – when did he last have a shower?), Alice explained what had happened. She'd come out of the supermarket with a loaded cart and was astonished ('thrown' was her word) to find a young Black man sitting in the right-hand front seat of her car. He didn't say a word while she bundled her plastic bags onto the back seat. Then she got into the driver's seat, and asked him please to leave. "I don't know who you are, young man, but you're in the wrong vehicle, you've made a mistake, and you should be wearing a face-mask anyway." To cut a long story short, the man cleared his throat and said in a rough voice "My name's John. I need help. Somewhere to sleep tonight. You didn't lock your car. You should always lock your car." "I almost laughed," Alice said. "He was so insistent. He just wouldn't get out of the car. So I decided to humour him and then get rid of him, so I said 'You sound like you have an English accent, John.'" "Yorkshire" he said. "Not the Queen's English. Better. My Mum brought me to Canada, my Dad left us when I was five, and then she went off with one of her boyfriends when I was sixteen, and then I got into a bit of trouble with the law" – and so on, a long story, and he absolutely refused to get out of the car! "Just for the night" he said. "I got nowhere to go, I won't go back to the shelter, they steal everything from you, and beat you up, and I can do things like taking out garbage and clearing snow when we got some snow."

Well, the upshot is that John (surname? and I thought Oh oh, a second John: the first one killed poor Ken and nearly killed Jennifer; what will the second one do, murder all three of us women in our beds tonight?) The upshot is that John2 is snoring (I can hear his snores!), as he sleeps warm and comfortable in a bed in the basement. And somehow I felt cheerful and hopeful, as I'll tell Chris when I reply to his email. John2 was actually polite tonight and expressed thanks to Alice and did the washing-up. So – well, we'll see! In the past, I would have been agitated and fearful, even called the Police while he was in the shower. But now – Christmas, and Alice, and the survival of Jennifer, and especially, maybe, the arrival of Chris in my life; also the possibility that COVID will be vanquished after all, following the amazingly-rapid appearance of vaccines: I give thanks to God for that, and for the hope that humanity will, after all, survive (are you hearing me, Boris?), and then will set about urgently remedying the harm we have created around us for so long.

Yes, but poor Jennifer has suffered a double loss – of her child, and of her child's father. A shocking, unexpected, painful and undeserved blow. But Chris is with her, helping her in her pain, giving her his support, his kindness, his generosity, his *love*. Thank you, God, for that too.

Anna: Sunday 13th December
I found his email this morning, and read it immediately – or as immediately as I could manage, in a short break from the current needs of our little community. Oh Chris, so wild and yet so generous!

Hi there, Wise Old Woman! Good to finally talk to you last night. I should have emailed you before, during the past few days, but it was all so tense – and I didn't want to be away from Jen – and whenever I had to be, because the Doctor wanted to examine her, I just felt so tired and worried. Anyway, Old Lady (well, *you* called yourself that!), she's going to be all right!!! The loss of the baby was a blow, but the Doctor had warned me earlier that, after what she had suffered, it was a real possibility. "She's physically fit and strong, but – " "Well, I didn't tell you before, because she asked me not to, but that man who abducted her hurt her very badly. After he shot and killed her friend Ken, and dragged his body into the bush, and then pushed his truck into the bush too (I guess only a few vehicles went by on the highway – and travelling too fast, probably, to notice what was happening) – Jen was too shocked and frightened to move at first, and when she did get out of the car and start to run, he came after her, and that's when she fell and must have hurt the baby in her womb as well as herself, and then he pushed her into the back seat of the car and drove off fast. About fifty kilometers further on, he turned off onto the road where his car was found later, pushed off the side, not very far from his property. He made her walk there from the car and locked her into his basement – where I found her a couple days later. And that's the whole story more or less – just so you know what happened and don't bug me for more information, hey! I am so sorry for Jen, what she's been through. She's been so brave and, as I think I told you, she was even concerned about John, that's his name, that shit – who killed Ken and abducted her, and all for what? Of course we'll never know now. But Jen *refuses* to see him as a villain, "It was horrible what he did to poor Ken, who was only wanting to help him, but he is still a human-being, Chris, and we can't know what was in his mind, what was driving him, and now he's dead and we'll *never* know, and maybe he could have repented and -" All in bursts and gasping while I tried to calm her. Well, that's beyond me, trying to forgive and even sympathise with a murderer, she's a much better person than I can ever be. I love her. But I can't say – well, *my* struggle is that she lost her child, who I told her I wanted to be *my* child too, I wanted to be the father after I married the mother! – She says she loved Ken and I'm sure she did – but now – Well, Wise Woman of the Woods and Waves, what do *you* think? No, don't think I want you to be responsible for what I decide! It's my decision, and maybe hers if she wants that. But your opinion – may be valued by your friend Chris.

Now I've replied to Chris, after giving Alice an abbreviated account: we are both so relieved to know that Jennifer is recovering and in good hands, especially Chris's: Alice was impressed, as I have been, by his faithful support, so important for Jennifer as she recovers from the physical and mental pain she has had to endure – and after her double loss, her baby and Ken, its father.

"She will have to be so strong" Alice said. "I wish we were closer – but in this COVID situation even that might not have helped much. How does that young man, Christopher, stay there at the hospital, what about the rest of his life? You said he's a graduate university student, didn't you, but of course all the universities are barely functioning now. Well, I hope we can meet him once all this COVID Lockdown is over, whenever that will be – seems sometimes that it'll go on forever."

I tried to explain the full situation to Alice, but I could see that she was distracted by our domestic situation. Maria is fine, according to Dr Gilbert, who visits more frequently now, as the time gets close; and her husband is with her through the night: he often makes her a small meal and tea (I think that's what it is) and helps her to and from the washroom. We also sometimes meet in the kitchen, he and I, and smile at each other.

But John2 is a different matter! Not that he's objectionable in his behaviour: in fact, he's surprisingly courteous and helpful. And of course, now that he's clean and has been outfitted in Boris's clothes by Alice, "he looks very respectable" as my Mother might have conceded. Even maybe handsome. I guess part of the problem is just that he's *around* all the time.

He clearly isn't used to that; he doesn't *read* (even a newspaper) and isn't interested in local news and any politics (say, about the COVID pandemic – I tried to talk to him about that, and he just smiled). I suggested to Alice that she could ask him to clean the car and tidy the basement, both needing attention! That seems to work, at least for the moment. And another thing I notice is the tension (is it?) between him and Alice; they seem to avoid looking at each other. And there doesn't seem to be any pressure, on either side, for him to move on. Well, I'm not *stupid,* Alice! So we'll see.

When I got a chance, this afternoon, I emailed Chris – replying to his email, mainly. After I had had my daily walk: it gets dark so early these days, especially with the heavy cloud (weather forecast warns of snow tonight. Of course, that will make another area of work for John2 – I think I'm beginning to think of him as a handyman, and that would give him a secure position in this household. Is that what Alice wants?).

Anyway, my email:

Hi, Sir Christopher: May I think of you, more respectfully now, as a Knight Errant who is serving his Princess to the very utmost? No, I'm not being sarcastic, Chris, I do honestly respect all that you have done and *are* doing for Jennifer – and so does Alice, who joins me in sending our deep, very genuine gratitude – we just wish you could also bring her here on your white charger for the forthcoming Christmas non-festivities – sorry, ignore the white charger.

I'm very grateful, too, for all the information you have given me about her dreadful ordeal following the death of poor Ken. Her bravery and sheer good-heartedness are truly inspiring. And her suffering and loss make one grieve deeply.

I wish I could express love and admiration for her better than I'm managing here, but I know you will add your kindness and generosity to what I'm trying to say. Oh, Chris – but knowing you are there for her, literally, is a *huge* comfort for Alice and me. You are our Hero! Please give Jennifer our deepest love, and say we're thinking and praying for her. (Which I *am*, Chris, more than I ever – Well, I'm *really* praying again; as I never expected to do. Though I do still often start by saying or thinking "Dear God-if-you-are God". And I pray for you too. In spite of our Tomfoolery (Chrisfoolery?), I think we do respect each other. Or I respect *you*.

So what else do I have to say? Actually, there's quite a lot happening here, in this old Toronto house that Jennifer would remember well. We have three guests: the young immigrant couple from the East (Syria), have I told you about them? – and now a young Black beggar who got into Alice's car and *refused to get out*! Oh, you have no idea how much is happening here! I'll tell you more if you are interested and have time to read it, but you probably have more than enough on your plate: looking after Jennifer, dealing with your family etcetera – and University work? (Alice and I wonder if you are a university student? I think you might have said that; but my memory is increasingly sieve-like, alas. In fact, I'm now wondering if I told you all that about John2 in our telephone conversation?)

So, my dear Christopher, let's keep in touch. Alice and I would be so grateful to know how things are working out for Jennifer, and for you. Please tell her we'd love to hear from her when she feels up to it. (I wonder if the Police gave her back her iPhone? It has a few messages on it from me! Ancient messages now. I guess she could email me on your iPhone or email?)

Our love to you and Jennifer – Alice and Anna

TWO

Anna: Monday 14th December

So, a new week opens. Less than two weeks now to Christmas Day! It's dull and blowy this morning. I'll get out for a walk in the neighbourhood before lunch, but meanwhile catch up with my record of – what? my boring everyday life, each day essentially repeating its predecessor and anticipating its successor: it's hardly surprising that unrest and suicide, two sides of the same coin, are increasing across Canada (I heard it on the CBC this morning – I still, thank goodness, have the little radio at my bedside that was a godsend during that Schubert Quintet week). The new vaccine has just arrived in Ontario (at Hamilton Airport!) and was immediately conveyed to Hospitals and Long-term Care Homes (for injecting 30,000 initial doses, to be followed by a second injection in a few weeks). I wonder when we will be vaccinated, Alice and I and surely Maria? Not that I think I am in much danger of COVID infection, but who knows? (Another item on the News: a big increase in suicides, especially of elderly men. Not surprising, I thought: so many of them are homeless – as John2 was.)

Also on the News, the American situation: nearly 300,000 Pandemic deaths, a 25% national unemployment rate; 3 million vaccine doses have arrived there – healthcare workers and the elderly to be the first recipients – but warnings from their health authorities that the current surge of infections is very likely to continue until 'herd immunity' is reached. Assuming that something similar is happening in other countries (I wonder about African countries?), maybe the COVID corner is slowly being turned and (listening, Boris?) the destruction of humanity will not occur – or *not yet.*

But the health authorities – at least here in Canada – are warning strenuously about the dire consequences of 'letting down our guard'. Will the 'presently-imprisoned' young actually restrain their desire for freedom (especially when that destructive lout, ex-President Trump, urges them on, for his hoped-for political benefit? I read an American political commentary recently that drew a parallel with Hitler's machinations to achieve power; but, for all the complications of the American electoral system, it seems that Trump will not be able to subvert it sufficiently so as to achieve permanent power). But so many uncertainties! What a dark time we are living in!

Anyway, enough of that. I'm only an ancient crone, Christopher, sir!

Anna: Tuesday 15th December
Some worry this morning about Maria. When I took in her rather-minimal breakfast (I don't think she eats enough!), I noticed that she was weeping, so I smiled in what I hoped was an encouraging way and said, rather stupidly really, "Won't be long now." I doubt if she understood what I was trying to convey, the birth of her child – but she tried to sit up and I realized that she needed the washroom; so I helped her up, and off the bed, and held her hand as far as the washroom door, which I opened for her. Because she was so tense, I decided to wait until I heard her flushing the toilet. Then she opened the door – rather hesitantly, I thought, so I went to her; she reached for my arm, and leant against me as I walked her slowly to the bed. Once she had settled, I gave her the tray with her porridge and milk. She looked at me directly then, and smiled rather tremulously. Because I wondered if she was in discomfort or pain, or even if the birth was imminent, I

decided to call Dr Gilbert – Alice was still away, having her hair done I think (I need that too! my hair is a mess, and I hate that!). Anyway, Gabriella the Midwife did come, quite quickly, examined Maria, and told me that the birth wasn't imminent, "but I'm glad you called me, looks as if it will be soon, probably next week, a few days before Christmas: I know you'll call me as soon as she goes into labour". When I retrieved the breakfast tray, Maria was lying on her back, with the bedclothes pulled up to her chin, and looking less tense. We smiled at each other again; how I wish we could actually talk to each other – that she had some English or I had some of her native language!

Then I had a telephone call from my neighbour Marnie in Hamilton. I had given her this number so that she could contact me if necessary, in any emergency or to give me any important local news. She's quite garrulous: nothing of importance, thank goodness, but quite a lot of information from the *Spec*, our local newspaper: that Hamilton has 150 new cases of COVID and altogether has had almost 800 cases now, with 5 more deaths; so Hamilton is now likely to join us in Lockdown. Of course, as I think I've recorded, the national campaign to vaccinate Canadians began yesterday: to quote Marnie, "it's the largest immunization campaign in the country's history, the *Spec* says, and the first lot of vaccines that arrived came through Hamilton Airport yesterday, so, when I saw that, I called my doctor but his secretary said it'll be months and months and months before I'll be able to be immunized, so I guess *we're* out of luck, we'll all be dead by then, what do you think, Anna?" Actually I think it's all amazingly good news (vaccines produced and being spread around the world within a year of COVID's appearance!). But – things could go wrong: so much in life is unpredictable, and also the world is in an uncertain and dangerous state at present. Alice and I watched the TV News last night: the new US President, Biden, looks and sounds like a good man who wants to unify his country after Trump's disastrous destructiveness and incompetence; but it won't be easy, especially as Trump will still be around causing havoc – will he ever Concede, actually accept that he lost the Election? I doubt it; he's actually a Traitor, I think! And COVID is still raging down there: over 3,000 deaths in one day, nearly 300,000 deaths in all so far, over 100,000 Americans in hospital! We Canadians must hope and pray that the border protects us, as far as possible.

When I went to bed, quite late and feeling exhausted (Alice and I, in our brief discussion after the CBC News last night, decided that she would take primary responsibility for looking after John2 and I would take responsibility for Maria, and of course she will be nearby, to give me guidance if I need it, and we'll always keep in close contact) – I was actually feeling quite anxious and unsettled, so I decided to read for a while in bed; and of course I now try to pray (using the Compline) before I go to sleep. Actually I found "Journey of the Magi", the T.S. Eliot poem, quite disturbing. It doesn't end very positively, to say the least: well, it does say "Grant me thy peace", but then "I am tired with my own life and the lives of those after me, / I am dying in my own death and the deaths of those after me." Oh – but I've copied those lines down to think more about the meaning later, but my immediate response, in the context of COVID – well, those words seemed, at the very least, bleak. Bleak. But the first Compline prayer, "for a quiet night and a perfect end", was more comforting, and then Psalm 31, "In thee, O Lord have I put my trust ... Into thy hands I commend my spirit ..."

Actually – I should also say, to be honest, that I have worried about the possibility that I and especially John2 may have brought COVID into this house (I was wearing a mask before I came inside after driving here, but he wasn't, and he still doesn't, in the house of course, though Alice gave him a mask and told him he should always wear it outside, and inside too if he goes anywhere near Maria).

Another of these dreary wintry days; trying to snow, but not with much success – a good thing. I wonder if John2 will clear the sidewalk when we do get some snow? Oh – and I didn't think to ask Marnie if her teen-age son will clear mine too, in Hamilton, when he does theirs after a snowfall, and I'll pay him later, when I get home after New Year's; must remember to call Marnie and do that.

Anyway, it's late-afternoon now. Nothing more to record, unless Chriscross calls – maybe he will, later. I always forget that they are a few hours earlier than us, there in the West. I must address the Christmas cards I brought with me – Alice will post them tomorrow when she shops, she said.

Anna: Wednesday 16th December
Now just nine days until Christmas. It used to be a time of such joyful anticipation. I remember how Jennifer and I bought a Christmas tree at our local supermarket, and loaded it into the back of my car, and set it up and decorated it (with mostly the old ornaments I inherited from my Mother; my Father asked me to take them after her funeral). Jennifer loved helping me decorate the Christmas tree. And of course we had a good fire going in the fireplace! And the neighbour-hood kids and their parents came and sang carols, it was a fine clear evening, and we gave them mulled cider and cook-ies! But this Christmas is so different. And Jennifer – I've

been thinking so much about her; it would be so lovely to have a good long talk with her! And see her. I wonder how she's doing. Hopefully she's recovering fast now from her wounds and from losing her baby. Poor Jennifer! A very different Christmas for her this year. For all of us! If only Chris would call or email! Maybe he will tonight, and if not, maybe I'll ask Alice if I can call his parents in Vancouver, I have their number from when Helen called: they will probably have the hospital's number and know when it would be a good time for me to call.

And I have just found an email from ChrisChross – I shouldn't make jokes about his name, but he always provokes me into a silly state. You're an old woman, Anna, act like one! (I can hear my mother saying that; she was always a bit humourless and censorious, in the best Maritimes tradition; of course life *was* hard for them when she was growing up; and she never really relaxed and let her hair down!) (I guess I'm making up for her? You're a bad influence on me, Mister Wiseman Junior!) Anyway – his email:

Hi there, Mother Goose: Just a few words, that's all I have time for – the doctor & his crew are on their rounds & will I know spend more time than necessary with Jen, she's so beautiful & smiles so radiantly & charms them all with her wit (could I be influencing her???). I know what you want to know, CrossCrone, and Yes, she's improving so fast (physically – no improvement required otherwise), & it really does seem that she will be ready to travel to Beautiful BC with us next week, for Christmas & New Year's & to live with me forever – better believe it! & now I should leave *you* & return to her bedside. Did she ask me to send you her love? I've forgotten, but I'll send it anyway – and *here it comes*!!! And so, Farewell from Your ForeverFriend Chris.

What a wild wit of the west! And silly sometimes. But Chris, you too will grow old. After many years of happy marriage to the woman you love, I hope! Yes, I've lost her, but maybe you will allow me to nurse your beautiful brood one day (one day *soon* because Time is catching up with me!). So I replied:

My dearest Jennifer and Christopher: Thank you for your email, Chris. My deepest love to you both. Have a glorious Christmas, enjoy every moment of it. I will be thinking of you! And thank you both for all the happiness you give me. I hope 2021 will be a year of joy, good health and fulfilment for you. Anna and I will drink some of her wine and get somewhat drunk in honour of your friendship.

And that will end this day's scatty record. Apart from my uncertainty about John2, I think all is well in this household for the moment. Maria is settled for the night, with her husband beside her. Anna and I have said good-night. All the lights are turned off and the rather noisy heating-system is keeping us comfortable. But – well, it's John2. Alice said she had given him a key of the back door ("Well, I want to make it clear that we trust him, and he can come and go freely. He's been helpful tidying the garden for winter, which I would have done earlier if Maria wasn't needing attention and support – thank you for taking that over – And I think his self-respect is important, don't you?"). But where is he? I made sure I cooked enough food for supper, but there was no sign of him. Should I go down to the basement and check? But – And I don't want to interfere and maybe cause trouble. So – to bed, Anna!

But more stupidity! When I opened my old Eliot *Collected Poems* to read "Journey of the Magi" again, I realized that two pages of the book were stuck together (not badly, but so the lines that troubled me are not from near the end of that poem but from the next one, called "A Song for Simeon"). But the real end of the Magi poem is also puzzling (to me, anyway): the Speaker asks "were we led all that way for / Birth or Death? There was a Birth, certainly ... this Birth was / Hard and bitter for us, like Death, our death. / We returned to our places ... / But no longer at ease here, in the old dispensation, / With an alien people clutching their gods. / I should be glad of another death." And I would be glad to *understand*; I know I'm not clever enough to follow Eliot's thoughts, but if I try hard enough – and would it matter anyway? So I put the book aside and tried to fall asleep – with that final line repeating and repeating itself. "I should be glad of another death."

But finally I fell asleep – and actually slept well. I have added that. And I'm adding this also, on Thursday morning, in honour of Beethoven, whose 250th birthday it was yesterday (according to the CBC). I would play a piece of his now, in his honour, a day late – but I don't have any of his music for violin here: I didn't bring any, only Bach; and it's more than unlikely that I'd find any in Boris's collection; for some reason none of us members of his Quartet knew, or could even really guess, he was always very unwilling to include any Beethoven in our performances. I remember that poor Ken badly wanted us to perform one of the late Quartets; and I wish now – "Sentimental, Anna", Boris would have said dismissively, that we *had* played the glorious Opus 130 (once – badly), which I love, just as Ken did!

Anna: Thursday 17th December
Yesterday I forgot (deliberately?) to record the latest information about COVID, gleaned from CBC news, and

Marnie. Things seem to be getting very bad, scary. In Hamilton, the Seniors' Home where I used to volunteer is being closed, after several COVID deaths. And most of Europe will now be shut down, it seems, over Christmas; and in Canada there is growing concern over whether hospitals, as well as their staffs, will be able to cope with an expected surge of new cases (850 yesterday, a record number). Lockdowns in Ontario will be extended and others imposed. And of course the American situation is even worse: the highest number now of cases in any country, I think. So – gloom; which the CBC and other media are clearly trying hard to counteract with Seasonal Cheer. But the initial euphoria across Canada, as the first doses of vaccine arrived and were hurried to hospital staffs and seniors, is dissipating; and we are informed that most of the population will have to wait until well into 2021 for their jabs. And what will the situation be like then, here and around the world?

Just for the record, I guess, here are yesterday's Ontario COVID figures that I gleaned this morning: More than 40 new deaths yesterday – more than 4,000 deaths since the beginning of the Pandemic, over 2,500 of them in long-term-care homes – currently nearly 1,000 Ontarians in hospital with COVID, over 250 in intensive care and, of those, over 150 on ventilators. Scary! The American COVID situation is of course far worse than the Canadian. But I'm not going to try to record the North American COVID disaster any further: it's beyond my capability, as well as profoundly distressing and worrying. Vaccinating is just starting in the U.S., and apparently it will not be completed in Canada until half-way through 2021! Meanwhile, there are actually many (how many?) reluctant or refusing to be vaccinated, some claiming wrongly that 'herd immunity' will automatically cure the disease. And surgery cancellations and delays are now more common. What a frightening mess we're in – while doctors and nurses struggle on, exhausted and sleepless: our heroes – but even heroes are vulnerable.

On the other side: the polite cheerfulness of neighbours. I drove to the local drugstore earlier today (it's not far, but I went there by car, once I had cleared off the snow – mainly to give the car some exercise); I needed to buy some small items (toothpaste etcetera; oh and chocolate, which she loves, for Alice). Masked, we customers lined up, socially-distanced; and it was notable that everyone was making an effort to be very cheerful and helpful. Yesterday afternoon, with John2's help, I hung up a string of celebratory Christmas lights, in the two trees on each side of the drive-entrance; I had noticed them when helping John2 to tidy the basement soon after his arrival. Most houses along the street are decorated with cheerful strings of small coloured electric light-bulbs, an old custom.

But John2. We had had quite a heavy snowfall during the night (the first one of this Winter, after some snow-showers earlier), and I was surprised when I went down for breakfast that John2 wasn't out helping to clear our section of the side-walk, and the driveway and the two vehicles. Alice had told us that she needed to go out this morning for her monthly INR (blood-check) at the local medical clinic, and of course I went out later. But no John2! I was thinking of going down to see if he was still asleep, when a police-cruiser turned into the driveway. To cut a longer story short: the two (masked) po-licemen were indomitably polite; and then I noticed John2 slouched in the back seat. Did I know this person? Did he live here, as he'd told them? Apparently the Police had been called to deal with a disturbance in a local bar late last night; and the instigator, very drunk had been kept overnight in a cell of the local police-station. Yes, I said, he does live here. Oh. They seemed relieved to open the door for John2 to emerge. He was not looking in best condition: torn jacket etcetera. I didn't want to discuss the situation with him (Alice did later) and he shambled off and must have spent the rest of the day in bed in the basement.

Of course I had to give Alice a brief account of what had happened. "Let's talk about it later" she said. "There's Maria to see to first. When I looked in on her earlier, after Joseph had left for work, I thought she was pale and possibly upset, and I wondered if they'd had some disagreement. Could you – she clearly feels much more at ease with you, Anna." So the day proceeded, and here I am towards the end of it; and I wonder how many others, in all the houses around us, in all the dwellings of Toronto, of Canada, of the wide world, feel as I do: that days and nights just slide and slide into each other, unseparated by the variety of activity that once filled our lives? So today is yesterday or tomorrow. And then silence, sleep. Immobility. Is this what life felt like in the past – a grey slope towards death? Sliding, sliding. Steeper and steeper. Oh, oh – stop, Anna. I will now return to sanity by playing Bach on my violin. Then it'll be time to make the supper etcetera. And I will read more T.S. Eliot in bed – not "Journey of the Magi", I'll come back to that later, but *Four Quartets*. "Time present and time past / Are both perhaps present in time future, / And time future contained in time past." And he didn't even experience a Lockdown!

Anna: Friday 18th December

Sunny! Brilliantly sunny – and the snow, still layered quite thick on gardens and driveways, but no longer on trees, is sharply reflecting a white glare. It's just a week to Christmas Day!

And what is happening with Jennifer and Christopher? I'll send him another email this evening, just to remind him that there are other people in the world – and some of them care deeply about Jennifer's wellbeing!

The Doctor came this morning, quite early, and spoke to Alice and me after she'd examined Maria (who seemed again calm: she smiled at me when I gave her the breakfast I had prepared – she actually seems to like the porridge I make, with apologetic memories of my Mother's insistence that no-body should ever *ever* face the day porridge-less!). The Doctor was quite happy with Maria's state of physical and mental preparation, wanted us to know that the arrival of the child is now fairly but unpredictably imminent, and some preparation was needed on our part: after telling us to be ready to supply bowls of hot water etcetera, she clearly also felt the need to check the ability and potential support of two elderly childless females, and so added encouragingly that "It should be an easy birth, she's young and healthy. You'll call Gabriella as soon as her waters break, and she'll come straight over. You have my telephone and iPhone numbers. Maria thought her husband might not be in attendance, and in my view that's a good thing." (I think I've made her sound more severe than she actually is.)

Then there is the problem of John (I'll drop the 2 now; that was rather silly!). As I said, Alice discussed that situation with me – in the kitchen, away from his ears (he was cleaning our two vehicles, inside and out, at Alice's suggestion). But what is the resolution? "He actually suggested that he should move into my bedroom! I was shocked when he said 'You have two beds in there' – he must have explored the house while we two were in the kitchen making a meal, maybe that's why Maria was upset. Anyway, I told him that wouldn't happen, and he said 'It's because I'm Black' and I said 'No, it's because you're a *man*' and then he said 'It's because I'm a servant' and I said 'No, it's because you're a man and still a *stranger*'. But then I had a brainwave, and told him he could have Boris's study – he used to call it his music-room; and there's even an old couch in there: Boris used to have his "forty winks" on it every day after lunch in his later years. John and I inspected it together, and he pronounced it acceptable. And it's far enough away from Maria's room to avoid disturbing her at all – I hope. So that's settled, at least for the moment; but there might be further problems, so be warned. There's the alcohol, and maybe drugs, I don't know – but so far, so good." I thought there was more than a hint of satisfaction in her voice: maybe, after the death of Boris, she has been deprived of challenge and satisfying authority? Well, for the moment anyway, this house and its inhabitants are calm.

Then there was a telephone conversation with Helen Wiseman. Alice was fine with that, "It'll cost hardly anything, just call them when you want to" she said. Because of the time-difference, it was their lunchtime when I spoke to her. She said all seemed fine, Christopher had said he'd be in touch with them if there was any problem; and he'd mentioned that he would be emailing me soon – so if there isn't an email by mid-day tomorrow, *I'll* email *him*. Helen also spoke about Jennifer being with them for Christmas and said how much she and Noel had always liked her, and implied that that they even hope for a marriage – "Christopher really must settle down, all that pop-music and wild living, Noel wants him to get serious and join the company, he says it's time, long past time". Of course, Jennifer and Chris are cousins – but does that matter these days? It certainly did when I was a girl, I remember my mother's shock when two locals who were cousins got engaged and then married – though I think they belonged to one of those newer denominations of which little can be expected!

Now it's after five o'clock and I'll make the supper (a rice-dish tonight!). Alice brought in a huge turkey the other day, for Christmas of course (most Christians can't conceive of a Christmas lacking the slaughter of turkeys, alas: turkeys bred in the millions, fattened by drugs, barely capable of motion, all for joyful Christian consumption – what do you think of that, God? I hope Alice is going to cook it; as a vegetarian, mostly, I'd prefer not to cook it, *or* eat it.)

But the CBC News I've just heard was again very disturbing. The Ontario COVID figures are beginning to look disastrous: 2,000 new cases, 40 new deaths; Hamilton to join Toronto and other areas in Lockdown on Monday, as hospitals and medical facilities are reaching breaking-point – cancelled operations, neglected diseases, more Seniors' Homes infected and isolated, exhausted and reduced medical staff – where will it end?

Anna: Saturday 19th December

Another grey day. Which is appropriate as Hamilton has now been designated a Grey Area and will join Toronto in Lockdown on Monday (for four weeks). That information from my Hamilton neighbour: I called her this morning just to check that my house still stands tall and safe – and, of course, to have a chat about the COVID situation. She says that there have been more local outbreaks, and closures of Seniors' Homes (including the local one in which I used to volunteer as a Friendly Visitor: despite great care, most of its

Staff as well as a good many of the resident Seniors are now infected); and she says that there is also a severe COVID outbreak in the local prison (as in other prisons: the inmates, in over-crowded cells, are very vulnerable; I used to volunteer in that prison a few years ago and remember how, even then, over-crowding and its consequences were a problem). So the conversation was somewhat depressing! But at least it was good to learn that none of my neighbours and local friends has fallen to COVID. So far: I have also learnt that I am not likely to be vaccinated until halfway through next year! Will we even be alive then? So many deaths already, in this society as in others.

The news is generally gloomy. A new strain of COVID has emerged in the U.K., with who knows what implications; their Lockdown is to continue through the whole ?Festive Season. Meanwhile, other diseases and increasingly-urgent medical needs are being neglected, for lack of attention in. And in several countries in Europe and America (notably of course the U.S.) infection and death rates are very high. There's a feeling of growing panic – isn't there?

I mentioned some of these facts and worries to Christopher when I sent him a brief email after lunch. He responded quite quickly, and this is his email:

Hi, there, Grandma Grumps (– *I was briefly annoyed by this*, as no doubt he intended: I see myself as, if not sunny, at least patient and equable!). Sorry to have been unnaturally silent for a while. Jen is doing well, the doctors say so, & I concur! She is noticeably more in contact with the world, and with me, her patient lover and admirer. We have even been walking, & talking about our future & her past (yes, you feature quite prominently, but only as grouchy slave-driver). She says she has forgiven you, & has asked me to give you her love, & best wishes for Christmas & the New Year. When we'll both be in Vancouver – my Father says he will be sending an airplane from his fleet to collect us in the next few days (well, I'll be honest, it's a small plane, a Piper Cherokee I think, if it's the one I once flew in when he & I explored Northern B.C. a couple years ago – so it's quite old but still feisty, like you!). (I lied, Dad doesn't own a fleet of airplanes – they belong to the Company & are used for business trips to the Far North mainly.) (When there is some business! Not so much at present!) Anyway – nothing much else to report at present. Stepmother says you called her earlier & she gave you our news generally. Oh yes, since you asked, about COVID: we do wear masks & Jen says I look like Zorro (who he? I didn't like to admit my ignorance – If you send me the answer in your next urgent communication, I will give Jen ten kisses from you!). Carpe diem! Kriskros

What else has attempted to give shape to this dreary day? After a short walk in the neighbourhood, I played some Bach, if only to keep in practice; but of course I enjoyed it, and so did John, to my surprise – he suddenly appeared and sat listening for a while. And then I read some more T.S. Eliot: "Marina", the last of the four *Ariel Poems*. I remembered how the word 'Death' recurs ominously four times in it. And a boat being launched: 'What seas what shores what grey rocks and what islands / What water lapping the bow ...' and that final evocative image of a 'woodthrush calling through the fog'; I remember how disquieted that made me feel, and yet also ('O my daughter') somehow at peace, as if I was being called to embark on a necessary voyage. An important journey. Perhaps I was. My life has certainly been an unpredictable journey (or has it? I hear Boris questioning, as he always did. No doubt being briefly in his study earlier, with John, and near his cello and collection of music books, has made me think of him, and his role in my life). Necessary, desirable, hopeful? Or not?

Sufficient unto the day? I've said good-night to Alice, and Maria, and Joseph (who had just come in, looking very tired), and John. (I wonder how Joseph and John get on? But I don't think they've had much if any time together, so far.) Now I'll ready myself for bed. Somehow there is, for me, a deep sense of peace tonight, in spite of all the COVID worries. Yes, it's been a positive day.

Compline. O Lord, "illuminate the darkness of this night … and from the sons of light banish the deeds of darkness"; "protect us through the silent hours of this night, so that we who are wearied by the changes and chances of this fleeting world, may repose upon thy eternal changelessness …". Yes. I don't think I'll ever be a true Christian, but those words do give me peace. *Deo gratias.*

Anna: Sunday 20th December

I woke (on another dismal grey wet morning, but I didn't know that until a bit later) – I woke to that joyful "Baby Baluga" song, and an interview with its creator and performer Raffi Armenian; now of course an elderly gentleman, but as vigorous and optimistic as ever! What a delight! And this has unleashed in me a plethora of happy memories from my teaching-days. So I just lay there calmed and happy until the interview was over and I had to get up to resume my kitchen duties. Raffi excoriated Trump (good!), expressed hope in Biden (good!), and spoke warmly and optimistically to and about all the children who are enduring this Pandemic. And as I dressed and entered the day, I was suffused with joy. Joy! When the News told us that the U.K. was virtually shut-down in fear of the 'new strain' of COVID spreading there – and of course we already know that there are over half-a-million Canadian COVID cases, 15,000 deaths in all, 6,000 new cases, nearly 2,500 of these in Ontario – and so on, etcetera. (As I've said, I've stopped even trying to note down all the statistics; not just because it's hard to do that accurately, especially if you're the klutz I am, but because such knowledge just depresses one. History, historians, it's all yours! I'm gone – at least until, if ever, the statistics record cheerful movement, the coming end of COVID.)

But what I do want to record now is cheerful. Cheerful? Yes, because another door has been shoved open for me. Christopher started all this! His cheerful slaps woke me up, I think; started me thinking and reacting positively; made me recognize how depression had become a defensive habit, when what I need is optimism and a calm positive mind. 'Baby Baluga' jolted me further, this morning, into recalling my past positively. The news, all those years ago, that I was being 'let go' – Well, it was beyond a shock; it seemed to undermine my whole existence; so *unfair*, 'I am a good teacher and colleague, you know I am: dutiful, popular, sensitive, the children love me!' 'It's the Recession, the Government, it's Politics, an attack on the Union (yes, I had been Secretary of the local Branch) – well, all of that, and more. Mort (the H.M.) told me how deeply he regretted 'having to do this', and he would support my becoming a supply-teacher, and he did keep his word. But supply-teaching, so insecure and so little real relationship with the kids, so *demeaning*! Well, 'needs must' I told myself, but if Jennifer hadn't come into my life, transferred from another school into *my* position, so it wasn't easy at first for either of us, but we made it work after a while, became friends, played some Bach together, and then – well, the Quartet was *also* a life-saver for me, nothing could have made me give up playing in it; even as second violin when I *knew,* and knew *he* knew, that I should have been first violin. And when Boris announced that we *must* play the Schubert Quintet (which I loved too) but we would need an extra cellist to do it, I knew it had to be Jennifer. I was afraid that he would reject her if he knew of my connection with her, so I got James to recommend her (in fact, Boris knew, or guessed, about my involvement, but I think now that, knowing his life would soon end – actually already *arranging* that it would end, with Dr Galbraith, under the new legislation) – Well, and especially with the arrival of COVID in Ontario just as we were starting to rehearse the Quintet for our next concert–

But why am I writing all this? Who could ever care about the details of my unimportant life? But maybe I just had to clear out my stale destructive memories. Now that my life seems to be rising again towards optimism and pleasure! Just as the COVID Coronavirus spreads its tentacles around the world. Bad timing, Anna! Or is it? We'll see.

So. It's 10:30 and I'll go to bed soon. A pleasant almost-cheerful day (except for the gloomy COVID news: London under virtual Lockdown now as the newly-identified 'very fast-moving variant of the coronavirus' has provoked a dangerously panicky exodus; oh, etcetera). I feel relaxed, almost optimistic. Surely, Lord, you will not impose suffering and death on Your people – well, You have, but please – I'll avoid TSE tonight and read Compline again – and again.

We had a light lunch, and then I went for a walk (round and round the garden, since the Toronto Lockdown prohibits, I think, the longer neighbourhood walks I would prefer). I became aware of John's nearby presence; he seemed to be watching me, so I approached him, and asked how things were with him. "Oh, I'm good" he said. "Just need some exercise, like you. Can you show me how to work the player?' 'You mean the one in your room? I don't know it, but I guess you just put a CD on the – Better, I'll come and see if I can avoid wrecking it – just as soon as I finish walking." He smiled – which I hadn't seen him do earlier. The clothes he's wearing now, Boris's, fit him surprisingly well, I was thinking; and altogether he seems more at ease, certainly less aggressive. He looks almost handsome! After we had persuaded the CD player into action, he asked me to choose a CD, and of course I chose the recording of Schubert's Quintet. "I'll have to leave you to it now, I must go and help Alice with the evening meal."

The meal was a great success. "It has to satisfy different tastes," Alice said. "And one person won't eat meat, which is a great inconvenience." She smiled at me. "But for tonight we have fish and chips, which I will cook to perfection, while you struggle with rice, carrots, and cabbage, so let's get on with it; and afterwards, a delicious fruit-salad with ice-cream; and I will also be simultaneously cooking tomorrow's main meal, a superbly tasty stew. So – and I bless my luck in having such great help, please lay the table, Anna, and inform John that he is in charge of the washing-up." Why was Alice in such a good mood? Why was I? It was altogether a memorably happy occasion. Joseph arrived just in time, ate his main course with Maria (who had seemed more at ease every time I checked during the day), and then joined us for dessert. He and John were a bit tense with each other at first, but relaxed after John told Joseph that a spider was crawling up his back:

much laughter, back-slapping. And then John was asking Joseph about his and Maria's long, difficult and dangerous journey from Syria to Canada.

Yes, it was all good today. Was that partly because I had relaxed too? Maybe. And I have just realised, too, that I haven't been worrying about Jennifer. But she and Christopher are in my thoughts and prayers.

THREE

Anna: Sunday 27th December 2020

Oh, oh. Once again (second time, better-be-last time!) I have lost a chunk of my precious writing, a whole week's record of my life and thought, beginning Monday 21st December. At least I know now why that happened! (On the first occasion – see the second section of *Quintet*, which is the first part of this Trilogy – I was left in outraged confusion: four days of the diary I was keeping with this laptop computer, while we rehearsed for our great COVID-19 Performance of Schubert's Quintet, simply *disappeared*: Monday 20th to Thursday 23rd of April etherized! And, immediately after the Performance, Boris died. A difficult time for all of us survivors – Alice, Jennifer, James, Ken and I. And now only Alice, Jennifer and I are still alive – and poor Jennifer was badly hurt when she and Ken were attacked.) Anyway – I will now have to try to recall all that happened in the period just before this Christmas, and right up to now. I think I will end my record (if I can even call it that!) at the end of this benighted year. On Thursday 31st December! So – Now proceed, Anna, and try not to scuttle the listing ship. (Second World War metaphor, why? Because I grew up hearing it, I guess.) Now get on!

COVID: My impression of the moment is that the concern over the new strain of COVID that emerged in England and South Africa has lessened, and the widespread vaccination programmes are giving some hope that, by the end of next year anyway, the Pandemic will be over. We hope – we all hope! Meanwhile, the destructive effects of COVID around the world continue, with worries that overburdened medical facilities and overburdened medical staff will result in a frightening collapse. We must hope and pray that won't happen. The Canadian figures that come to me from CBC reports etcetera remain disturbing: so far, over 500,000 COVID cases, and nearly 15,000 deaths. So, Provincial Lockdowns – the Ontario one has just started and will last four weeks. And the situation in the USA and in some other countries is even worse. (As I type that, I wonder if I and others are becoming optimistic without sufficient reason: and if, as time moves on, we will become dangerously complacent. But then, I'm a worrier: like my Mother, as I may have said already!)

Anyway, next topic: the Christmas Eve fright and then relief over the airplane mishap involving poor Jennifer and Christopher on their way to Vancouver. She had been pronounced well-enough recovered from the effects of what she endured as a result of her kidnapping, and then of the loss of the child I didn't even know she was carrying. Poor, poor Jennifer. Maybe if Christmas hadn't been looming, and if there hadn't been pressure from Chris and his parents, the doctor and hospital staff wouldn't have allowed her to leave, before Christmas – who knows? Anyway, the plane crash (thank goodness, it happened not very far from that hospital) was not so very serious, or that's what Chris told me in his short email on Christmas Day. It was a small plane (a Piper

Cherokee, I think he said) but also quite old, used by his father Noel only for short flights, to board-meetings etcetera, and it was piloted by an old friend of Noel's who had been an Air Canada pilot before retirement a few years ago. He was to spend Christmas with them, after they landed at the private airfield on what I gather is the very extensive Wiseman estate. Anyway, it seems that the poor man had a heart-attack, but still managed to land the plane safely, thank goodness, on a minor country-road, and Chris radioed for help almost immediately. I'm sure that Helen and Noel Wiseman had a bad shock – as I had when she called, very breathless, to let me know what had happened and to say she and Noel were just setting out by car. "We'll bring them home for Christmas, they sound shook-up, and poor Hal, the pilot, he's an old friend, they got him to the hospital as quickly as possible, of course, but oh, he died on the operating-table, Noel says he had struggled a bit with his health after his retirement, but nothing serious, and we'll miss him so much, but at least Jennifer and Chris will be home with us." And that night Chris called himself and just said they were all right, but Jennifer was exhausted and his Mother had insisted that she needed sleep and should be in bed, she could call or email later. But she hasn't called yet and I hope she's all right. It must have been another terrible experience – after her abduction and imprisonment and the loss of her baby. I'll email Chris again and maybe call him later – I don't want to worry them after all they've gone through, and I know he conceals his emotions, but he must be – it's almost two days later now. How lucky they were to survive that accident! I'm glad I didn't know about it until afterwards. That was nearly another very sad situation for Alice and me. And meanwhile, here in Toronto –

Yes, I wrote about it in great detail, and now that's all lost! But of course my memory of it is still fresh, and it was such a joyful occasion! John had a lot to do with that. I said earlier how he just appeared in Alice's car and wouldn't leave – and we're now so glad that he's with us! At first, Alice said, she thought the worst, and she was ready to call the Police. But then – something about him, and I can see what it was: he was filthy when I saw him first, and he was also rude and seemed unpleasant: we were actually a bit frightened of him, Alice and I. Anyway, Alice took a chance, as she told me later, and once he was showered and dressed in clean clothes that had belonged to Boris, he seemed to be a different man (or boy – he's just nineteen years old, he told us later.) Of course he'd been in jail for I think stealing, he didn't want to talk about that – and after he had suddenly left us and gone back to the bar near the supermarket and spent another night getting drunk etcetera (where did he get the money from?), he told the Police when they arrested him in the morning that he was living in this house with his family, and so they brought him back here, I guess to see if he was telling the truth, and I said he was; so they let him off with a severe warning. While he was showering, Alice and I talked about what to do; I said I was a bit frightened of him, but Alice was convinced that he's fundamentally 'a good guy' and he'd never attack us and she thought we should give him another chance (to be honest, I thought she was being foolishly indulgent – as if he was the son she'd never had). And then she experienced (as she later put it) a sudden inspiration: to let him have Boris's study as his room; and that really seems to have worked, because since then he has been generally friendly and helpful, with Maria especially, who seems to really like him – and in fact Gabriella the Midwife, who delivered Maria's baby daughter in the early hours of Christmas Day, said he had been an indispensable help, those were her words. He and Joseph get on very well, too, and also with Joseph's uncle and his two cousins, who came to see the Mother and Baby on Christmas Day! Oh, so much rejoicing – and eating and drinking and conversation, and really getting to know each other, and celebrating together. I think it was maybe my best Christmas ever! And we all probably almost forgot about COVID! Alice said to me (it's clear she's very tired, she did so much over Christmas) that we must talk about John, and Maria and Joseph and their little daughter – she's such a happy smiley baby, hardly ever cries! Later today, maybe, we'll talk – Alice is out shopping at the moment.

And I don't think I mentioned that I'm teaching John how to play the cello – or rather, the basics of that, he'll need a real cello-teacher: but he seems to respond very immediately and fully to music, has a natural feeling for rhythm especially, I think. It was really a brainwave of Alice's to give him Boris's room; I can see he's happy there, and helping in the kitchen etcetera – and especially happy helping Maria with her baby. So all is well at the moment, *very* well – thank you, God; I haven't been praying with Compline or reading any more TSE for a while, too much else to do! But I will, tonight.

Also, thinking about COVID as I have intended: things seem to be going from bad to worse, alas, at present; what with the new highly-infectious strain spreading fast in the U.K., and even starting here in Ontario, where the daily number of infections has been over 2,000 for over a week now. And of course there are continuing increases elsewhere (in the U.S. for instance), and growing concern about the ability of hospitals, already overcrowded with COVID cases, to cope. It's almost a relief to learn that the U.K. and the Common

Market have reached a deal (just in time!) for their future relationship after Brexit happens in the New Year.

Anna: Tuesday 29th December

A glorious sunny morning has dawned! I got up a bit late (I'm getting lazy!) and once dressed etcetera went (masked of course) to see Maria. She is not only well-recovered (from what? I think mainly worry, and of course she is naturally shy) but, especially when holding her child to her breast, seems to glow with happiness and pride! It's wonderful to see how transformed she is! We smiled happily at each other as I sat down beside the bed, and tried to communicate benevolence, asking the baby's name; but, apart from her shyness barrier, I think Maria really doesn't understand English much, if at all (her husband does, a few words at least, probably because his brother and nephews have been giving him informal conversational lessons before and during the Lockdown). But when the baby stopped feeding and closed her eyes, I asked with gestures if I could hold her, and Maria smiled Yes, so I stood beside her and she raised her to me. And – well, I can't describe the emotional effect, but it was a sort of ecstasy combined with sharp regret that I never had (and of course never will have) a child of my own. Then I handed her back, still thank goodness sleeping contentedly. And went about my kitchen duties.

After which, I went for a stroll in the garden. There is still quite a mantle of snow, not on the trees any longer, but on small plants and the path (a bit slippery, so I was careful) – and of course on the deck, where we often gathered for breakfast and conversation in Boris's time. 'Boris's time': yes, it does seem now to have been a different era, before COVID really struck hard and transformed (deformed?) our lives.

Attuned with the morning's sunlight, the radio news was dominated, as I woke up this morning, by reports of the successful dispersal of the anti-COVID Vaccines, in Canada and around the world. Apart from some glitches (here in Ontario, for instance, and in some so-far-deprived areas), the 'roll-out' seems to be operating quite efficiently, creating an almost-euphoric reaction. Obviously sheer relief is a dominant cause. *But* there are warnings about the destructive effects of complacency. I telephoned my Hamilton neighbour over breakfast, and she quoted from an article in the local newspaper: some very troubling Canadian statistics (over 15,000 COVID deaths since the Pandemic started, for instance) with a warning by an infectious-diseases expert: we must all remember that "This is a deadly disease" and that hospitals are already full and their staffs exhausted. And also the new variant, first identified in the U.K. and South Africa, is causing confused concern.

Altogether, after that immersion in today's news, I was glad to get outside into the sharp sunlight and totter around Alice's garden. ('Alice's'? Well, it is; Boris left it all to her; and she fully deserved that after her years of serving him. But I do – admit it, Anna! – I do feel occasional jabs of – what? Jealousy, regret? I think I need some more TSE and Compline to purge my mind of any and all resentment. Yes, Boris did hurt me, in his rejection, and often unfair criticism; but, to some extent at least, I accepted, even needed, his negative treatment – or did I? So complicated. I was young, impressionable, cut off from my Nova Scotia roots – Once, when I was still in my youthful 'religious phase', I remember a priest, after my monthly Confession, telling me that I was too self-centred, I should try to be more focused on giving Service, etcetera – Well, I tried to – Oh, Anna, stop this! At your age! I remember my Mother saying, with exasperation, "Just get on with it, Anna! There's a lot to do around here – have you fed the chickens yet?' I guess she was right; I guess they were *all* right. And anyway, too late now – just move on!

Well, forgive that diatribe, dear Imaginary Reader. (I should obliterate it – in memory of my two losses of self-expression on this malignant machine, oh the cruelty of this World! But I won't – now that I know how to do it, if I want to! Yes, Anna, that's what we all mean about you: stupid, arrogant! Obliterate these words and all of this Record, forever? Just Opt for SLEEP as you take a break from your ever-spewing text; then SWITCH OFF THE ELECTRIC CURRENT; easy, easy! Almost as easy, Boris, as ending one's life, with legal medical support? Maybe, one day soon, I'll try that.) Sleepy befuddlement!

Well, proceed – I'll proceed. About John. And Alice. Is it jealousy? Anyway, she said, yesterday afternoon, just after lunch, while he was playing the flute (very well, I thought – he has a natural musical ability: he's also managing to play Boris's cello better and better, without any teaching!) – she suddenly said "Can we talk, Anna? About John." And of course I said Yes, so we went to her room.

"I can see how helpful he's being, Alice," I said, pre-empting her. "He's doing so much around the house, and clearing snow, and – "

"Yes" she said, "And even cooking – that lamb-stew was great! And Maria – helping her. And Joseph obviously likes him too, and trusts him. She always smiles when John's with her, and she walks about leaning on him – even before the baby was born; he showed her she *must* keep active – and he's so good with the baby, even changes her nappy sometimes, did you know? Well, of course you would – and you've been so helpful with her, too, Anna, we'll all miss you so much when you go home." (I had told her I thought I should leave here on Thursday, New Year's Eve.) "But about John – he's been so *very* helpful, don't you think? Who would ever have guessed that would happen? He was such a trouble and a mess when he came: you'll remember how I just wondered how we could get rid of him, as soon as possible, and if it hadn't been almost Christmas – And you know, he's been talking more about his early life, how his Father would beat him, hurt him, for no reason; and then his Father disappeared, in England this was – and his Mother came back to Canada: did you know she's Indigenous, First Nations? – and she took him to her Reserve, but he didn't like living there, and seems he got into some trouble, with drugs or whatever, and he ran away, and that's how he ended up living on the streets here in Toronto, stealing and begging and maybe even selling drugs, just to survive – So no wonder, when he saw me leave my car-door unlocked – Well, you know the rest, and *you* have helped him too, Anna – and I know he appreciates that, he said so – But" and she looked hard at me, "now we have to take a decision. About his future. And mine. You'll be going back to Hamilton in a few days, you said – and Joseph's Brother told me – *his* English is good, and he said they expected that our three guests – he meant Maria, Joseph and their child – would soon go to live with him and his sons (his wife, I gathered, drowned when they were crossing the Mediterranean from Africa) – Apparently he and his sons had expected that when Joseph and Maria reached here, as new refugees, they would live with him – But something frightened Maria – she misunderstood something one of them said, and apparently thought Joseph's Brother was going to have her sent back to Syria – We noticed how nervous she was, even in this house after we welcomed her and tried to make her feel at home. Joseph's Brother told me that in Syria she had been in the local market trying to find food for her family, *begging* for food, because apparently they were penniless and nearly starving – when there was an air-raid and her home was bombed and her whole family were killed. Well, as I was saying, she was still very frightened and confused when they came here and I took them in, the two of them – Joseph had been a friend of one of her brothers in Syria and so he had become her protector after her family were killed, and they fled together, in a huge crowd of refugees at first, and finally on their own, and somehow (he wouldn't say how) they reached England. And then Toronto. And then *here*. After meeting Joseph's relatives, as I said. Sorry if I'm repeating myself, and confusing you."

"But why did they come to this house, Alice?" I asked. "I've wondered about that."

"Oh, apparently Joseph somehow had the name of an old friend of Boris's who knew that I'd done some work helping refugees, a few years back – and of course *he* gave them directions to this house. But Anna – As I said, I want to talk to you, just for a few minutes, about John. Of course the main responsibility is mine, you have just been very kind in your relations with him: he appreciates that, Anna, as I mentioned – and especially about helping him play Boris's cello and flute, and you told me, didn't you, that you think he has real musical talent. So now – well, I know he wants to stay on here, at least for now, and into the New Year – and I have no problem with that. I guess I'll have to fix things with whatever authorities, but one of Boris's old friends is a lawyer and he said any time I need legal help – So really I guess I'm just asking if you have any thoughts or opinions, I know you care very much for him too, and you've helped him, and encouraged him, with his music, and cooking, and – well, generally. I remember that at one point you spoke in his favour when I was, well, quite negative about him. So -?"

"Oh, Alice – thank you for saying those things. But you know, I think it's very clear now, especially after all his hard work and all the help he's given – yes, as you said, he's a fine young man – he truly *is*. But the rest is up to you, and him. If I can do anything useful, to help, well, 'Just let me know, Old Lady!' – as Mr Christopher Wiseman would say; *if* he was in a good mood! And Alice, I really should call Chris or his Mother – he's another charming, talented, helpful, handsome young man!"

Probably more was said, and we were both quite emotional, I think – but that's enough; most of what I've recorded (tried to remember!) about this conversation between Alice and me gives a fairly accurate impression of what was said – I hope. Otherwise, why am I spending precious time recording it? No, don't respond to a childishly naked appeal for approval! (If you are reading this private diary!!) Now, let me see if I can get out of here, this computer, without blowing its contents up and away. (A Second Disaster? One was more than enough, Old Lady.")

Good! I'm safely back. And now: Jennifer. Please! I am so longing to hear from you; to have a conversation, after so long, after so much worrying, so many happenings in your life. At least it would be good to hear from Chris, or his Mother, or even his Father. So –

Well, it wasn't Chris who answered the phone, it was his Mother – but at least she said in passing that he had mentioned (how long ago?) that he was going to send me an email. Really, the young cannot be trusted! Anyway: Helen. She started by saying, to my alarm, that Jennifer had "given them a fright", during the night after they got back to their home in B.C. on Christmas Eve. "I think she had a nightmare, which I guess is not surprising after all she's been through, poor girl. She was screaming, and both Noel and Christopher woke up, as well as me, and as Chris was closest, in fact he was in the same room, he got to her first and tried to calm her, and eventually she just burst into tears, poor girl, and wept and wept. So it wasn't the greatest Christmas for her. I made them a herbal tea, and Noel and I went back to bed and Chris carried on just talking quietly to her until she fell asleep. And both of them slept through most of Christmas Day! Well, until the afternoon. In a way, it was just as well that we are all in Lockdown, wherever one is in Canada, or feeling that we might as well *be* in Lockdown! So it was a Christmas we here will definitely all remember! I hope your Christmas was a bit calmer."

Well, enough. I'm off to bed. It's getting late. But I have Boris's TSE and my Compline. Will peruse both until my eyes droop, and then I hope to enjoy a good night's sleep! Yes.

Anna: Wednesday 30th December

A dismal day! Grey, wet; most of the snow washed away. But I did have a good sleep; though I also had a dream about Jennifer – not a nightmare: she was smiling and walking towards me, arms raised to embrace me, and then she was gone; why wasn't that a disturbing dream, even troubling? But it wasn't.

I had read "Little Gidding" again, the last part of *Four Quartets*, "With the drawing of this Love and the voice of this

Calling ... the children in the apple-tree / Not known, because not looked for ... Quick now, here, now, always ... And all shall be well and / All manner of thing shall be well ..." And finally I just read the Compline Prayer for the Epiphany: "Thou hast appeared, O Christ, thou Light of Light: unto whom the sages offer gifts, alleluia, alleluia, alleluia." Which I repeated a few times and then fell asleep.

Tomorrow I return to my home in Hamilton. After breakfast, I called my neighbour to let her know. She said all was well; but that there is a continuing concern about the growing number of COVID infections and deaths there; the hospitals barely coping, and several recent deaths in the local Seniors' Home (where, as I've probably mentioned, I used to Volunteer). Very disturbing news, every day now, she said. And increasing concern about the general COVID situation in the City, and also a big increase in drug-deaths (opioid-overdoses): she read for me parts of an article in yesterday's local paper, to the effect that there is a 'surge of COVID patients', nearly seventy, in the local hospitals, with well over a thousand 'active cases'. Well, as she said, "What can't be cured must be endured" – an old saying of my Father's, I was surprised to hear it! But I hope the Vaccination programme *will* be a really effective cure, and then, after apparently a year or so, COVID will be defeated. Let's all hope so!

And then an email from Chris was suddenly there. I had been hoping, so much, for one from Jennifer, while knowing that, from what Helen had told me last evening, it wasn't very likely. At least I knew that Chris would be fully aware of how worried I am – and especially so after his Mother told him about my call. This is what he emailed:

Hi there, Anna! Jen & I send our love. I know you are

worried about her (StepMother told me earlier about your call last night). Jen would of course like to talk to you but please believe me when I say she really isn't in a good state yet – you've heard how she woke up screaming during the night before Christmas – and after that it was a long while before she could get back to sleep. I have to say that my esteemed Parents behaved very well, Dad would normally have thrown a fit and immediately got wildly drunk (oh, all right, I'm not being fair: I can feel your frown!), but they both just let us sleep through most of Christmas Day, & then we've been taking everything very quietly & calmly since then. Of course my parents managed to connect with our useless old doctor, who advised rest & sleep, he actually gets paid for that crap! Dad tried to bribe him to visit, but he was made of stern stuff, & his wife, clearly a Harridan like one I know, was probably standing on guard right beside him, breathing heavily. Are you listening, & believing me? Upshot, dear Old Girl, is that I have just checked with your somewhat somnolent Friend, who is lying beside me, & she sends her love to you, says she has little to add to my admirable epistle, & looks forward to talking to you soon. (You told StepMa that you're going back home to Hamilton tomorrow, so we will call you there tomorrow, I promise – Drive carefully!!! And watch for Off-duty Cops on the make!!!) Your Secret Admirer & Lord of the Boondocks, ChrossChris

Yes, typical Chris. But I was just happy and relieved to know that he and Jennifer are safe, after all their (and especially *her*) travails. So now, I'll go on a masked stroll round the neighbourhood before lunch, and then I hope to have more time with Maria and her baby, as well as John. Final opportunities! Parting tomorrow will indeed be such sweet sorrow. But life is composed of such. Isn't it? Especially for the Old. Rehearsals for the Final Exit.

John's cello-playing is amazingly good – considering he hasn't yet had a lesson. Alice said he mustn't form bad habits, and she is in touch with a good teacher, one of Boris's old students, who lives nearby and told her he might either come here or have John go to his place for lessons in the New Year; and John is clearly eager for that. He's also playing the flute with increasing expertise: Maria loves him to play gentle melodies for her, and her daughter crows with delight when he does! In his rather abrupt, self-conscious way, he thanked me for, what? being a good companion, I guess – after I had thanked him again for cooking that memorable Christmas lamb-stew, so enjoyed by all of us. (In fact, that whole meal will be remembered, I think, not only for the food, including Alice's delicious fruit-salad, but also for its *bonhomie*, the crackers we pulled (thoughtful of Alice to buy them!), and the champagne, or wine, or fruit-drink, or tea, with which we drank to the health and happiness of our families and friends; and we were very aware, Alice and I, of the deep emotions in the guests: not only in Maria, Joseph and his Brother and Nephews, but also in John, who was probably thinking of his Mother and his friends on the Reserve or the streets of Toronto or incarcerated in various prisons. I wondered then if anyone would make a speech; but nobody did; I think we were all just full to bursting with a deep contentment.)

Then, yesterday, I spent time with Maria and her daughter. The child now seems quite ebullient, a happy contented little creature who crows and splutters with apparent delight. The joy of being alive! A line (from I think Shakespeare) came into my mind – "What a thing of beauty is man"? – oh, that's not right; I've forgotten it; which happens more and more frequently – no, it's come back: oh – no, it hasn't! Soon we'll need to get a buggy (or Alice needs to) so Maria can take the baby out when warmer days arrive. Spring!

Anna: Thursday 31st December

I slept well, and as I woke turned on the little bedside radio: and caught the end of some interviews with people who had (heroically, without question) kept on working right through the Pandemic; and then, after the News, there was a heart-warming joint-interview with a brother and sister who were just reunited, just discovering each other, in late middle-age (their father had left his son's mother without knowing she was pregnant, and his second relationship had produced the daughter, and neither of the siblings had known the other existed until, through a coincidence I can't remember, now, so many years later – ! Their delight sounded authentic, and their intention to get together as soon as the Pandemic is over). It was good to hear such joy, such a positive account, as this sad year ends. For the Pandemic won't be ending for a while – I caught on the News the facts that, in the U.S.A. yesterday, there were 3,800 COVID deaths and a record-high number of the infected in hospital. And here and elsewhere around the world, the suffering caused by COVID continues: 3,000 new cases in Ontario, nearly as many in Quebec, and I forget how many deaths. So, as 2021 looms, dare we hope for the positive change promised by the new Vaccines and the renewed endurance of populations? Boris, are you there, watching over us? Even now, with a maybe-renewing Christian faith, I can't be confident that you are. Oh – no more of this. "You so stupid, Anna!"

So now I am getting ready to leave. Yesterday I was able to get some of my clothes washed and dried (Alice has a washing-machine and drier in the basement), and now my suitcase is packed. I have had a quiet breakfast with Alice, and spent a happy hour with Maria and her baby (still un-named, I think?). But Maria is increasingly active, recovered from whatever physical and emotional stress has been (not surprisingly!) troubling her so deeply. Joseph looked happier, relieved, last night when I bade him adieu! And after John comes in for lunch I hope to have a final chat with him (I think he's helping an elderly neighbour at the moment: Alice suggested that, and the neighbour has already telephoned her thanks).

2:30   And now I'm back in my Hamilton home. It felt a bit stuffy at first (well, of course it did, Anna!), but now, with the air being circulated better after I adjusted the furnace fan's setting, it almost feels normal again. And *I* do, too – feel more normal, if that's possible. The highway was no problem, though the traffic was heavier than I expected (why? People returning home who shouldn't have gone out?) The weather sure ain't great, but could be worse: cloudy, breezy, a bit chilly; almost all the recent snow has now gone (but more is predicted for the weekend). I called my neighbour, to thank her for keeping an eye on my house while I was away, and she said it had been no trouble, the whole neighbourhood has been "quiet as the grave, it's almost spooky"! And I said that was obviously because I was away, but she didn't laugh – clearly my neighbours don't regard me as a 'barrel of laughs', any more than you do, Chris?

And right on cue (how did that happen, Boris? Your little joke?) the phone rang. "Hullo, hullo, is that the Hamilton House of Horrors?" I told Chris that was feeble and far-fetched, but he was already chattering on. He said he was calling, rather than emailing, because he had, right there beside him, a lovely languishing Lady who unaccountably desired to converse urgently with a wretched raucous Wrinkly (what is a Wrinkly?) whom she faintly recalled encountering during an earlier stage of her life – "Oh, just stop your stupidity and hand the phone over to Jennifer." Which he did. And the first joy was just hearing her voice, after so long and after all her undeserved suffering. And then – well, we both just wept for at least a minute before we could talk. I can hardly remember what we said to each other. But one thing I do remember. And that is "Anna, Anna, we're going to get married in the New Year, just as soon as COVID is over! Chris wanted us to get married now, *right now*, but then we couldn't have any guests, even you – just his parents; so we must wait, but Chris says – "And then he grabbed the phone from her and bellowed "Did you hear that, Old Crone? I *proposed* and she *accepted*, and the rest will be *joy*." So – deafened, "Well," I said, "then that's another reason to hope and expect that 2021 will be a better year than this expiring one – the best year ever!" I actually said something like that.

And afterwards, I thought about one other thing: what she, and then Helen later, had told me about Noel's apparent attempted rape of Jennifer, which had caused her to flee B.C. not long after she came to Canada as an immigrant; I remembered again how she had been so upset, so troubled, by her memory of that episode. But now – well, I hope all that turmoil, and her suffering, then and now, can be put behind them. I hope she told Christopher, and I hope they have both spoken to, and forgiven, his Father, explicitly or implicitly, preferably explicitly, so they can all move on. Yes, I do think, I do hope, I do *believe*, that forgiveness is best. And another quotation came into my mind: "After such knowledge, what forgiveness?" Does that come from *Four Quartets?* I have just skimmed through my copy of the whole poem, without success. But, oh the conclusion, to "Little Gidding", to *Four Quartets,* I read that again: "... all shall be well and / All manner of thing shall be well / When the tongues of flame are infolded / Into the crowned knot of fire / And the fire and the rose are one." Yes, he's quoting Dame Julian of Norwich there, again; but the rest – the final three lines? I remember how they puzzled me in the past. What do they *signify,* the fire and the rose? Masculine and feminine? Destruction and creation? Movement and stability? Ugliness and beauty? Pain and joy? All of the above – or None of the above? Nothing. But "Nothing will come of nothing" (*King Lear* – I know that one!). And so – "We shall not cease from exploration". But I also yearn for *something restful.* The Compline, how it begins: "The Lord Almighty grant us a quiet night and a perfect end." Yes. I repeated that several times. Yes. Ultimate Joy.

So: I *am* near the end. The end of my diary, the end of this Year of the Plague. And my own imperfect end. God, bless us all.

But – Not so fast, Anna! I woke up this morning with my mind repeating one word: "Plague", which was also my original title for *Quintet;* and now that word was taking me beyond Boccaccio's *Decameron,* his record of the fourteenth-century Plague that he observed and experienced; it took me to Daniel Defoe's *Journal of the Plague Year,* his 'historical fiction' (1722) narrating experiences of a London resident during the Great Plague of 1664–5. And so – a final few words, as my Farewell. To *our* Plague Year.

Anna: Saturday 2nd January 2021

"In the end is my beginning." I must not despair. There is always chance and change, in this glorious confusing uncertainty we call Life. Or so I believe. As I close my chattering record of 2020, unsatisfactory as it certainly is, the statistics of this second wave of COVID, in Canada alone, challenge comprehension (Can they be accurate? Over 500,000 cases of infection, more than 75,000 of them active, and about 15,000 deaths, so far; in Ontario alone, over 3,000 new infections yesterday, and over 4,000 people in hospital with COVID, nearly 800 of them in intensive-care, with over 50 new deaths; and of course record-high numbers in the USA, with over 300,000 fatalities, and in countries like Brazil, and England, where the 'variant COVID infection' is reported as now "spreading at an alarming rate").

Yesterday delivery of my newspaper resumed, and I read that the President of the Ontario Hospital Association has just commented that "It seems like every day we reach a new kind of threshold that maybe a few months ago we thought was impossible. This pandemic is accelerating.... So these numbers are going to get a heck of a lot worse, in all probability."

Hospitals overcrowded, doctors and nurses exhausted; confused fearful populations: but the Vaccines – created, disseminated and administered with exceptional speed, are inspiring hope around the world. And so "all shall be well," Boris? "And all manner of thing shall be well"?

Anna: Sunday 10th January

Oh, oh – I thought I had finished with this limping Diary, BUT – Events have transpired (as they say), to jolt me into writing this P.S., this Epilogue.

One event above all: on Wednesday last, 6th January

(which, ironically, was also Epiphany – the Church Festival commemorating 'the manifestation of Christ to the Wise Men of the East'; I'm quoting this from my Dictionary) – on that day, what is being defined now as a 'violent insurrection in support of President Donald Trump' (whose term of office is to expire next week, when he will be replaced by Joe Biden) occurred – a failed coup? I watched some of the mayhem on television, and the media were of course full of it this morning. Trump has all but destroyed himself; so that, in the short period (two weeks?) before his successor is inaugurated, one can hope that he will not be able to take any further destructive actions. Apparently there were five deaths during the melee, and considerable destruction of property, as well as stealing of papers etcetera. That 'American democracy' has suffered such humiliation is of course delighting national enemies (like Putin of Russia, with whom Trump had a mysteriously positive relationship) and troubled friends (like our PM, Trudeau). Well, the consequences of what happened in Washington on Wednesday will be considerable and perhaps disastrous – but they belong to the future. (And will, I hope, include forceful criticism of the "exceptional nation" doctrine that has – in Boris's opinion, and I think he was right! – for so long disfigured American thought and action.)

Meanwhile the COVID news in Ontario, and in most Canadian Provinces, is increasingly disquieting. On the CBC News today: in Canada, over 650,000 cases, 83,000 of them 'active', and over 17,000 deaths; in Ontario, about 3,400 new cases, about 400 patients in intensive care, and 40 new deaths. (And much worse in the USA.) I have some difficulty hearing and recording these figures accurately; but the general situation, in this second phase of Canadian COVID, is clearly, and increasingly, *dire* (a word now widely used); and medical and

political authorities seem to be getting panicky. A curfew is starting in Quebec, and Ontario is likely to follow very soon. The situation in seniors' homes remains serious, with the disease still spreading in many of them; first doses of the Vaccines are being administered, but more slowly than hoped; and meanwhile the concern over hospital overcrowding, the exhaustion of doctors and nurses, and the forced neglect of general medical attention, and of diseases other than COVID, is intensifying; with current expectations that, following the recent Holiday Season (and the likelihood that many people disobeyed appeals to stay apart), a sharp increase in COVID infection is imminent. Meanwhile the USA has just "surpassed 4,000 virus deaths in one day". There seems always more COVID information being disseminated, most of it distressing, than one has time to absorb and report.

But a different, earlier disaster has been in my thoughts today. I had forgotten that, before COVID began to monopolize my thoughts, Ukraine Airlines Flight 752, which "included 55 Canadian citizens, 30 permanent residents and 53 more travelers bound for Canada", was shot down, exactly a year ago, by the Iranian military. Horrible, and also just one of the distressing disasters that dominated the news last year, and increasingly depressed our thoughts and daily behaviour. No wonder there was almost a sense of relief, even euphoria, when the New Year, 2021, began, and we could all hope that sorrow and despair will be succeeded, eventually, by optimism and happiness.

Well – Time to leave, Anna! For good. One quotation from Defoe's *Journal of the Plague Year* stumbles back into my defective memory: "We are all in this craft and must sink or swim together". Yes.